Advanced Praise for WALLY

"Unique in form, Don Peteroy's epistolary confessional road novella is compellingly poised between future and past, acceleration and reflection. Only through departure can Wally (and readers) begin to arrive at the complexities of desire, volition, and responsibility. Wally's cognitive detours through history, physics, psychology, and religion make his journey all the more rich and engaging."

~Chris Bachelder, author of *Bear v. Shark, U.S.!* & *Abbott Awaits*

"Early in Don Peteroy's *Wally*, the eponymous hero tells his poor wife, by letter, on the occasion of his fleeing to the Yukon, again, "don't try to get in touch with me." Unlucky for her, but lucky for the reader, Wally is himself an expert getting-in-touch-er, a grouchy, funny, anguished, eloquent observer of and reporter on everything that matters in the world, including himself. He's terrible company as a husband, but the best kind of company as a narrator."

~Brock Clarke, author of *An Arsonist's Guide to Writers' Homes in New England* & *Exley*

Cover Art © Brian Phillips

Book Design by Tina Holmes

First Edition Published by Burrow Press, 2012

ISBN: 978-0-9849538-1-3

Burrow Press
625 E. Central Blvd.
Orlando, FL 32801
www.burrowpress.com

for Seth Courtwright

WALLY

a novella by

DON PETEROY

Christiane

July 27, 2007

Thanks for supporting me tonight!

Dear Elizabeth,

I have with me ten pairs of underwear, three cartons of nicotine gum, the credit cards, Mapquest directions, and four partially crushed boxes of Cheez-Its. It's six in the morning. In thirty minutes, you'll read the letter I taped to the shower curtain. You'll call your boss and say, "I can't come in today. He's left for the Yukon Territories. Again."

This time, don't try to get in touch with me. My cell phone is off. I'm avoiding email, too. Instead, I plan to communicate with you the old-fashioned way: through hand-written letters. I'll send the entire bundle once my therapeutic journey is complete. They'll contain everything you need to know: dates, locations, epiphanies. I realize that this is one-sided and inconsiderate; I'd certainly be a better husband if I updated you in real-time, but the reason why I've chosen to withhold contact is simple: I cannot experience a psychic transformation if you're making me feel guilty about it. I'm dealing with enough remorse already, especially after what's happened and what I did last night. I want to become a man of dignity and honor, and in order to secure those virtues, I must avoid shame at all costs. One little, pleading email that says, "Wally, where are you? I miss you!" could destroy everything I seek to accomplish.

You're thinking, "Nice try. Remember what happened when you tried to pull off the same stunt four years ago? You won't even make it to the Canadian border before you get a flat tire, have a panic attack, and come home apologizing."

I know I'll reach my destination because, so far, I don't feel the sense of entrapment that thwarted my prior attempt to leave Cincinnati. I've thought this trip out. I'm clear-headed about what I'm doing. Even though that note I left on the shower seems frantic, my self-evaluation remains objective. Yet, despite how well I've maintained a healthy sense of skepticism, I cannot dismiss that there might be some greater, spiritual powers nudging me along. Every event that has transpired since I tiptoed out of our apartment this morning has proven, beyond any doubt, that the city wishes to extract me.

I'll explain.

I had some errands to run before beginning my journey, the first of which involved heading over to the Court Street Theater and getting fired from my job. It would have been easier to just quit, but I'm a forward-thinking person. You and I would probably need a few unemployment checks to hold us over until I found a more agreeable job, unless your sudden success started to pay off.

In order for me to be eligible for compensation benefits, the terms of my dismissal would have to fulfill Ohio's "approvable job separation" criterion. I'll admit, I only scanned the precepts in our employee manual, but I'm certain that unless I committed an act of theft, violence, or sexual harassment, I'd meet the requirements. The hard part would be convincing Kyle to fire me. You know how he is: Kyle rarely gives into people's demands without putting up a fight. He's a black-belt in the Socratic Method, both fearless and shrewd from all his years doing improvisational acting and debating liberals at town hall meetings. Although he'd threatened to fire me many times over the last two years, this would be different. My removal was on my terms, and therefore, he'd do everything in his power to keep me employed. He'd drill me with his rhetorical expertise. I'm not that keen; I'd contradict myself and expose my motives. So, I devised a strategy, one that would give Kyle no choice but to terminate me. I'd simply avoid direct confrontation. All I'd have to do is leave a note on his desk. He usually doesn't come to work until the early afternoon, and I'd be long gone, hopefully in Indiana by that time.

Last night, I spent an hour writing the note to Kyle. You were sitting right next to me, knitting a sweater for your mother's birthday. You were having a hard time maneuvering the needle, what with the food poisoning you'd experienced earlier that evening. You were trying to conceal your discomfort. Our discomfort. You didn't seem at all curious about what I was doing. You probably thought that I was making a grocery list.

Initially, I'd composed a detailed explanation of why I should be fired. I even lied, said that I may or may not have charged senior citizens full admission and pocketed the difference. My words were deliberately ambiguous. I'd written, "What with my bipolar disorder, I can't tell whether I committed these crimes in my imagination or not. Sometimes, when I'd get home from work, I'd find a few dollars in my pocket. Maybe that was change from Starbucks? I simply can't remember."

After you went to bed, I reconsidered what I'd written. Even though I'd used dubious wording, the letter's content could still be construed as incriminating evidence. I tried writing it again, several times, and finally whittled the note down to its essentials. The finished message said:

Kyle,

You've been a wonderful boss. I regret to inform you that I won't be coming to work for an indefinite amount of time, which could be anywhere between a week and a year. It would be in your best interest to fire me for this violation. I wish you luck in finding my replacement.

Sincerely,
Wally Tiparoy

When I arrived downtown it was a little after 5:30AM and still dark. I parked a few blocks from the theater because the Sanitation Department was spraying chemicals all over Court Street. According to the local AM radio station, a truck carrying a forty-foot-long tank of unprocessed milk had overturned. Court Street was ankle-deep in thick, curdling slime. The yellow river ran through downtown, and emptied into the Riverfront Stadium parking lot.

The stench was nauseating, so putrid that after one breath I felt like my stomach was full of warm mayonnaise. My nasal passages constricted in protest. Stray cats lined the curb, a meowing, goo-slurping ripple of fur and fleas. A few brave ones wet their paws. When they discovered that their lactose paradise was shallow enough to traverse safely, they jumped in and rolled joyfully in the muck. The policemen, standing behind flashing barricades, suppressed their laughter, while the Sanitation Department dispersed a mist of toxic absorbents from pickup trucks. Early morning joggers used their cell phones to take videos and pictures of the spill.

I rushed past newsmen in oxygen masks. Some were milling about, sipping coffee from Styrofoam cups while waiting for more pertinent news, like related deaths and car accidents. Other reporters deliberately lied as the cameras rolled: "Could this cause an E. Coli epidemic in Cincinnati? The EPA has yet to issue a statement, but stay tuned for tips on how to survive this potentially catastrophic event."

I unlocked the theater's front door. One of the framed advertisements in the lobby—for our upcoming performance of Chekov's *The Cherry Orchard*—was slanted. I repositioned it, moved the velvet ropes aside, and walked toward the administrative offices. Light spilled from beneath Kyle's door. I assumed that he'd accidentally left the lights on, so I pressed my key into the lock and turned the knob. When I opened the door, he jerked back and the wheels of his seat scraped across the tile floor.

"Wally!" he shouted. "What are you doing here?"

Damn it, I thought. Something must be wrong. Maybe we were being audited again? The IRS had come down on us last year, after I'd forgotten to renew our 501c3 tax exemption forms.

I thought to just drop the note on his desk and run, but a cluster of images on Kyle's computer monitor momentarily distracted me. Splayed across the screen, in flashing gold letters, were the words Cast Fetish Tube. A video showed a man performing two absurd tasks at once: he was rubbing his naked groin against a woman's leg cast, while sucking on another impaired woman's metal neck brace. My mouth opened, but I emitted no sound. Kyle had always seemed so prudent, so sexually conservative, the kind of guy who sprayed down the bed sheets with Febreze before and after sex. Yet, I'd always sensed that there was something off about him. I could never put my finger on it, but now the truth was exposed. You and I both know that it's always *those types*—the morally pompous Midwesterners who bemoan sexual liberation—who tell their wives that they're going to a church fundraiser and end up doing two-man acrobatics in a stall along some interstate, their pockets bulging with twenty-five cent condoms they'd purchased from the dispenser on the wall.

But cast fetishes? I had a hard time coming up with an impromptu Freudian analysis of this one. I bet you find Kyle's cast fetish shocking too, unless you've known all along that he's a pervert, and you've chosen not to mention it, which I'd find curious because you tell me everything about everyone's business. Such deceitfulness on your part would make me wonder what else you've concealed about Kyle. I've been wary about you and Kyle since you met him seven years ago, but I've always chalked it up to my deep-rooted trust issues.

When Kyle saw me gape at the screen, he said, "It's not what you think."

A band of sweat formed beneath his hairline. His cheeks turned scarlet. He stuttered, "You see, I'm working on an original play about a bizarre group of incidents. Historical incidents. Very bizarre." He rolled up his sleeves. "It involves, among many other things, a series of rapes in a hospital in Milan during World War One." There was a copy of Hemingway's *A Farewell to Arms* on his desk. Four, thick lines of cocaine were arranged on the book's cover. Another big surprise. I knew that after our performance's opening and closing nights he'd celebrate by getting buzzed off of a few beers, but otherwise, he wouldn't drink at all. When a fallen piece of scenery had broken his wrist during last summer's musical, he'd refused to take Tylenol 3 with Codeine, even though the doctor had prescribed it. "I don't want some junky narcotic in my system," he'd said. "I'll just be a man and suck it up." He'd thrown the pill bottle in the office wastebasket, and later that night, I pulled it out and took it home, much to the dismay of the actors who had similar plans. Thirty pills lasted me three days.

So there he was, snorting cocaine, engaging in one of the most expensive habits in the world. Another mystery solved. Last year, our auditor had discovered missing donor and patron contributions. All along, Kyle had said it was *my* lousy bookkeeping that got us in trouble. Now, I could see the truth: he'd snorted that missing 6% of our NEA grant.

Kyle continued, "This is my first attempt at writing a historical play. I've been working hard at it, day and night, as you can see."

I said, "I thought you've never written a play in your life."

He scratched his face. "Sure I've written 'em. I'm just careful about when I declare a project finished. I take my time, whereas *others* rush."

Kyle was alluding to my last play, *Did You See That?* You haven't read it because you've never read a damn thing I've written, except maybe my diaries. *Did You See That?* explores what would happen if all the mirrors in the world attacked us. The play was supposed to be a parody of modern self-consciousness. I'd entered it in the Cincinnati Emerging Playwrights Contest. Dr. Richter, professor of Dramatic Literature at Anderson College, was the contest's judge. He was also the Court Street Theater's principal consultant, financial advisor, and a longstanding Board of Trustees member.

Had I won the contest, you would have known about it. Or maybe you wouldn't have. It's not like you ever gave a damn about my art.

A few days after I received notification that someone else had won the contest, I asked Dr. Richter why he'd turned down my play. He said, "You're trying too hard, Wally. It felt, I don't know, like it was *written*? You need to learn how to let the drama unfold naturally. Your ambition keeps getting in the way." Incidentally, the contest had only three entries. The winning play was called *Climb With Moses*. It was about a mother and daughter relationship. The mother had cancer. The play was written by Stephanie Holt, a local librarian. It was the first drama she'd ever written, and it was autobiographical. *Did You See That?* was my sixteenth play. It came from my imagination.

I mention this because the world is unfair. I wouldn't be surprised if Kyle got as lucky as Stephanie Holt, if his cocaine-induced historical drama became an Off-Broadway sensation. He'd rub it in my face. He'd say something like, "Isn't it crazy how you've struggled for so long, while I just throw this shit together and boom! Instant success!"

Kyle slid his chair back to his desk. He placed a newspaper over the Hemingway book. He had a vegetable drink on a napkin, and his teeth were coated in chopped seaweed and spinach. His breath stank like a Hefty bag full of rotting cabbage.

He said, "Anyway, it's not even six in the morning yet. Why are you here?"

The air duct above us blew a sour milk scent. We both tried to ignore it, but couldn't. We wrinkled our noses. Without thinking, I reached into my coat pocket and pulled out my appeal for termination. I should have ditched that plan and told him that I was feeling sick and wouldn't be at work tonight. I could have just left, never come back, and he would have fired me. Kyle snatched the letter from my hand and unfolded it. He read it out loud. My eyes moved along the office walls, and I noticed things that I hadn't picked up on before. Not that I'd been in his office much—there was an unspoken rule at the theater: Kyle's space was off-limits. Taped to the wall was a creased and sun-stained Fugazi concert poster. His corkboard was empty, but for a single, curled-over receipt. But what really made me suspicious was the empty five-by-seven picture frame on his desk. I wondered whose photograph had been there, and why Kyle had removed it. Could it have been a secret lover? Maybe that's why he was so adamant about keeping us out of his office: we'd discover who he's screwing.

I could spend all day psychoanalyzing him, but let's face it: I was trying to distract myself. I hadn't prepared for the possibility that Kyle would be present.

He finished reading the note and laid it on the table. He pulled at his collar, then lighted a cigarette from a pack of Newports that sat next to his computer.

"Is this a medical emergency?" he said.

"Not at all."

"Then?"

I swallowed hard. I had to be careful. One misused word, one slight lapse of logic, and he'd jump all over me. I said, "I'm going on a therapeutic journey. I plan on taking my time, which will put the Court Street Theater at the mercy of my indifference toward professional responsibility, unless, of course, you fire me and promptly find a replacement."

He chuckled. "Did you and Elizabeth get suckered into one of those South American time-share things? Let me tell you about those—"

"I'm going to the Yukon, to the town of Inuvik. I'm not bringing my wife with me."

He took a long pull of his cigarette, then tilted his head upward and blew a plume at the ceiling. On the computer monitor, a video spontaneously loaded. There was a woman in a full-body cast, all but for a hole cut in front of her mouth and another near the anus. Two men approached her, and I turned my eyes away.

Kyle said, "Inuvik? Never heard of it. You've got family there?"

"No," I said. "The only thing worth seeing in Inuvik is Santa Claus."

"Right," he said. He lifted the paper that concealed the cocaine-covered Hemingway novel. "You want a line? I feel like you could use one right now."

"No thanks. I'm kind of in a rush to get out of here, so I need to know. Am I fired?"

He hunched over, snorted, then rubbed his nose. I swore that I could hear the cocaine sizzling in his sinuses.

He looked at his computer screen. The men were trying to remove the woman's cast with hacksaws. They were jerking off while they sawed.

Kyle took another drag off his cigarette and flicked the ash on the ground. "What does Liz say about your therapeutic journey? I mean, you tried this garbage once before. She wasn't pleased then, and I'm sure that now—"

"She doesn't know yet."

"I thought you'd taken care of all your little mental issues!

Jesus, Wally, she's bent over backwards to save your marriage, and here you go." He looked up at me. His pupils were the size of Tic Tacs. "She got you this damned job. You owe it to her. Do you know how hard she had to work to convince me that you'd be a good employee?"

"How hard?" I said. Through the corner of my eye, I glanced at the empty picture frame. "Did she fuck you?"

"For Christ's sake, Wally! I can't believe you'd even think that!"

His expression changed. He looked like he just completed a crossword puzzle that he'd been laboring over for a week. He pointed his index finger at me, accusingly. "I know what's going on. You haven't been taking your medication." He snorted another line, then wiped his nose with the back of his hand. "Tell me, are you off the meds?"

"I haven't taken my meds in months. Pretty stupid of me, isn't it? Especially since we agreed that if I was going to work for you, I'd take care of my personal issues."

He slapped the desk. The remaining two lines of coke scattered. "OK, you're setting us back. By weeks, really. The new season subscription forms, the refunds for *Hamlet*. I mean, you're seriously messing things up. We've got *The Cherry Orchard* opening and, look, here's what we'll do... I'm willing to forget about your little visit, to rub it off as some neurological short circuit. Just go home, take your Prozac, get a good night's sleep, and come back later and we'll make believe this never happened. In the meantime, I'll call Aetna and we'll find you a nice place, maybe one of those ten-day resorts for neurotics, and we'll get you out there next month when things slow down. It'll be like going for an oil change. In, out, and all better. Sound reasonable?"

"No."

He stubbed his cigarette out on the bottom of his shoe and threw the butt onto the ground. "Fuck, Wally, fuck! You can't do this!"

"Are you telling me that I'm fired?"

"Your wife's going to hate this."

"She's going to hate lots of things, but ultimately, it'll all be for the best."

"Uh-huh." He leaned back in his chair.

"So?" I said.

"So?" he said.

"What now?"

"You tell me, Wally. What now?"

"I'm leaving, and I can't promise you that I'll ever be back, so you can either wait on me or start looking for my replacement."

"Son of a bitch," he said. He held his hand out.

"What?"

"Give me the keys."

I removed the theater's three keys from my keychain and dropped them into Kyle's palm. As far as I was concerned, this symbolically signified my successful termination. That wasn't hard, I thought. Maybe Kyle was too high to put up a fight.

I stole a quick glance at his computer screen. The woman's cast had been removed; the movie was over. I said, "Do I need to sign anything, or can I just go?"

He lighted another cigarette. "It's unemployment you're after, right?"

"I wouldn't mind it, but no, I'm not that cheap."

He cracked his knuckles. His cold and critical glance pierced me. He knew. I could see it in his eyes. He'd known all along. He was just waiting, feeling me out, putting off the argument until I'd become confident. Then he'd smash me. "You know," he said, "I've always kept my politics out of work, but, in truth, I was hesitant to hire you. I had a sense that you were like all the other Social Security thieves out there. I mean, your résumé was shit, absolute shit. I remember looking at it and thinking, 'What a loser! Is this guy for real?' All these long lapses of unemployment. A month at Target. Three months off. Two weeks at Whole Foods. Nine months off. I'm curious, how long did it take you to squander your parents' life insurance? Were you able to sustain it for—what?—the last ten years, or did you blow it all at once?"

"Don't bring my parents into this. That's disre—"

"I remember the first time Liz had me over for dinner. I'd never seen so many video games in my life. Like I was at Michael Jackson's Wonderland."

"If you're implying that all I do is—"

"Your wife swore that you had good work ethics. She said you couldn't keep a job because you were selling yourself short. I was willing to suspend my disbelief, Wally. And for a while, you had me fooled."

He reached for his mouse, minimized the Cast Fetish Tube screen, and continued, "Just so you know, I'm going to do whatever I can to prevent you from getting unemployment. Ultimately, it'll be for the best."

Unemployment benefits didn't matter, anyway. We wouldn't be taking a massive financial cut, what with your sudden success. We've made more money in the last month because of your research than I've earned in an entire season at the theater. You and I both know that a year from now people will be writing about your research in *Scientific American* and

TIME magazine. The Discovery Channel will block out some primetime for a documentary on how the detection of the B-Gravitrope revolutionized modern particle physics.

Although my heart was thumping, I tried to sound cool and indifferent. "Do what you have to do. Go talk to Dr. Richter, if you must. I mean, he'll probably wonder what you were doing here so early, and I'm sure he'd be fascinated to know that the theater's manager snorts coke while jerking off to cast porn, but don't worry, I've got you covered. I won't tell Elizabeth about your secret life, either. You've still got her fooled."

"She's not as foolish as you'd like to believe."

"And she wasn't a fool for marrying me, as you'd like her to believe."

The only way to prevent Kyle from coming back with a witty retort was to just get the hell out of there. I took a step back, but before I managed to escape, he said, "One last thing. The moment you leave this theater, I'm calling the crisis hotline. I'm ethically obligated to do that. You don't seem well right now, and I have reason to believe that—"

"I'm not suicidal, and I'm not homicidal. That's all they'll care about. There's too much milk flowing everywhere for the police to give a shit about a playwright who hasn't taken his meds."

So I closed Kyle's door and stepped out into the lobby. What a miserable fucking place. I wouldn't miss it, that's for sure. I rushed toward the front door and walked around the velvet ropes and bronze banisters. After one last look at Chekov's silhouette on the advertisement, I headed out into the street where fog rose from the milky stream. I was done. I *am* done.

The stars flickered out one by one, and red sunlight bent over the horizon. Cincinnati's tallest skyscrapers caught and reflected the glare, sent it down upon the streets, tainted with the hue of metal and dirty glass. There were sparrows perched on power lines preparing to receive the first beams of light that broke above the river valley's hills. This early in the morning, the world looked glossy, like it was coated in wax.

Despite the closed roads and barricades everywhere, Joey's Authentic East Coast Wi-Fi Bagel Shop was still open. A mixture of all-night drinkers and hurried businessmen crowded the tables. I sat at a booth by the window and watched the people who were waiting for the bus. Behind me, a customer complained loudly to the kid at the cash register, "It's six-thirty, how could you be out of everything bagels?"

I bit into my everything bagel.

The customer went on, "Can't you improvise, for Christ's sake? I swear, your generation's lost the ability to be inventive."

The kid went and got the manager.

What's funny is the customer was right about our generation being pragmatically fruitless. I'm having a difficult time shaping this letter's rhetoric in such a way that I can convincingly avoid addressing significant concerns. I could sit here and transcribe every conversation I overhear, or attempt to reroute your attention by rendering poetic scenic descriptions, but whenever I try to direct your gaze elsewhere, I'm inadvertently enunciating what I've sought to censor. I've run out of inventive ways to circumvent talking about the real issue at hand. So let's stop dancing around what we both know.

I'm leaving not because of some vague want of therapeutic adventure, but because it's imperative. I've abused you, Elizabeth. We've made every effort to divert our awareness of the truth, but our apartment swells and creaks from the psychic weight of the perpetually unstated, unexamined. We've altered our rhetoric to avoid words with painful connotations. Whenever anything pertaining to spousal abuse appears on television, one of us seizes the remote. We've ceased listening to NPR. We've rid our bookshelves of memoirs, slipped them into the library's donation bin, those thin stacks of domestic traumas handed back to the public and growing more numerous every time one of us goes out on errands. We've avoided the music room.

Four years ago, I slammed the piano's key guard down on your fingers. That's what happened. It wasn't my medication; it wasn't a one-time neurological malfunctioning. My hostility was deliberate, perhaps even innate. You're a physicist, and you know damned well that nothing happens in a vacuum. Although we've made a silent contract that such a thing would never happen again, I can't guarantee it. Yes, a long time has passed, but malevolence wears a slow wristwatch. It's in no rush. My grandfather, Marvin, for example, was evil from the day he was born until he became an old man. He abused my father. He beat his wife. One day, when he was in his sixties, he snapped out of it. He behaved for seven years. Then, like a thief in the night, his wickedness returned, and he embraced it until he died. Those seven years were as quick as a breath across your face.

I know for certain that you frequently wonder why I did it. The answer that Dr. Dillman provided, the answer that we agreed to espouse, is hardly satisfying. Yet it's such a taboo subject that neither of us will discuss it, and have chosen instead to "tolerate" the psychological consequences. Ever since the incident, you haven't slept well. Every morning, you marvel over the past night's wreckage: the blankets twisted like braids, the bed sheet unmoored from the mattress, your pillows discarded on the floor as if you'd hurled them at some intruder, your pajamas damp from sweat.

You deserve an explanation, Elizabeth. That's what I'm trying to get at with these letters. What was going through my mind four years ago, what led to it.

It begins with Kyle. Kyle has always wanted to get you in bed. Let's recall the whole piano lesson ordeal, which instigated the chain of events leading up to my explosion. I remember the night when we had Kyle over for dinner. By that point, we'd known him for a couple of years, but we'd never had him as a guest. I was in a sour mood that evening. Although the two of you had packaged our get-together as an informal, friendly gathering, I smelled conspiracy. Kyle had come to check up on me. Just two weeks prior, I had embarked on my impromptu journey north, and, along with distressing you, I'd missed two days of work. Now he was in our apartment, making sure you were OK, and that I wasn't going to flip out and screw over the Court Street Theater again.

During our meal, Kyle berated the Unitarian church's musical director for hiring some third-rate pianist. He said, "I guarantee, if I had piano lessons, I'd outplay that twerp in six months."

You glanced across the dining room, toward the room where we kept the piano, my guitars and amps, and stacks of

CDs that we no longer listened to anymore. The piano was coated in dust. Ever since you embarked on the search for the B-Gravitrope that year, you hadn't had time to play music. You often expressed how guilty you felt for neglecting the piano—the piano that your grandfather, a Julliard graduate, once owned. The piano that he willed to you.

You turned to Kyle. "I can teach you."

"Oh, that's not necessary," he said.

You'd never offered me lessons.

"Really," you said. "You've done so much for me with the church, and Christ, you got Wally a job."

"You don't owe me anything, Elizabeth."

"Then consider it a gift rather than a returned favor."

His face brightened. So did yours. There was a light passing between the two of you. I reached for the salt and shook it over my carrots. You watched, nose wrinkling. "Gross, Wally," you said. "Salt and carrots don't go together."

I shrugged. "We're all trying something different tonight, aren't we?"

The conversation about the lessons resumed. What killed me were the logistics. You'd asked him what would be the best time and day for a weekly lesson, and—pay attention now, because you weren't paying attention back then—Kyle responded, "How about when Wally isn't home?"

I thought about how all it takes is eight pounds of pressure to rip a person's ear off. I knew what Kyle was doing: he was creating a scene. Here was a man who'd spent his entire life in theater. And when he wasn't in theater, he was fighting to make the world theatrical. He wanted narrative consistency. He wanted our dining room to be the focal point of a Neil Simon romantic comedy about a sexy, small-breasted physicist and a misplaced Shakespeare scholar who manages a community theater. The conflict: the physicist had mistakenly married a parasitic deadbeat.

Kyle continued, "It would make perfect sense to do it when he's not around. Wally's easily distracted, and he gets frustrated when there's a lot of noise. I should know. I'm with him eight hours a day." He chuckled.

"Totally. He needs quiet," you said. Then you added, "And, you know, I try to respect his privacy when he's working on playwriting. But sometimes the smallest noise will set him off, like the tea kettle, or the cat jumping off my lap and onto the ground. He's called me a *thought assassin* a few times. Once—"

I interrupted, "I don't mind if Kyle's here. It won't interrupt me."

Kyle said, "I take Monday's off, and Wally's scheduled to work Monday afternoons—"

I raised my voice: "It doesn't bother me if you're here when I'm here."

You said, "That's what you say now. But the minute he starts playing the piano."

Kyle said, "We're being considerate, Wally. We don't want to inconvenience you. Monday is best."

I shook salt onto my bread. "Look. Right now, it's Wednesday night. Mid-week break. We're both here. I don't feel inconvenienced. I usually just veg out on Wednesday nights anyway. I watch Star Trek DVDs or goof around on Xbox. So I insist, Wednesday nights."

He looked at you, unable to conceal his disappointment. You didn't look happy either.

"Fine," Kyle said, taking the salt from me and putting it at the other end of the table. "He insists. So Wednesday it'll be."

When you looked down at your plate, he flicked the worst kind of glance my way. I could read his face. It said, "You don't deserve to fuck her."

I reached for the pepper.

All these little gestures, all his facial nuances, all his rationalizing, all of his insistence upon my absence: it wasn't subtle. Does it now make sense why I slammed the key-guard down on your hand four months later, when you were practicing alone, after he'd left? The room still carried his odor, for God's sake. His K-Mart brand leather boots. The paint fumes that clung to his clothes from earlier in the day, when he was helping the set designers because they were behind schedule. His breath reeked of boiled herbs, and now the room stank of thyme, basil, and garlic. I sat down next to you on the piano bench—my intention was to be flirtatious and funny by interrupting your song with bad notes—and all I could smell was Kyle. Your neck emitted a parsley stench. I knew that he'd tried to make a move. He might have succeeded. Who knows? That's why I slammed the key-guard down on your fingers. Although I can't justify abuse, you would have done the same damned thing.

———————

What a relief it was when Dr. Dillman said, "Abusive behaviors usually start much earlier in life. One rarely becomes violent in his late twenties."

I caught your sideways glance traveling over the tissue box that lay between us on the couch. It was the first time you'd looked at me in two days.

He continued, "Sometimes psychotropic medications can amplify impulsive behaviors. Now—" he looked at his clipboard, "The last time we changed your medication routine was… three months ago. Went off the Prozac, and started on a half milligram of Risperdal, correct?"

I nodded.

"And you've been taking it once a day?"

"Yes. On a full stomach."

"Have you had any side effects?"

I hadn't, but I figured if we were going to blame my behavior on a pharmaceutical imbalance, I might as well embellish a few things. "I've definitely been on-edge lately. For about a month."

Dr. Dillman glanced at you. You said, "I agree. I've seen it."

I said, "I've felt nervous. About nothing in particular. Just nervous."

You added, "Not quite grounded. Always this distant look in his eyes. Restless. Can't relax for even a second."

Dr. Dillman said, "How have things been going at work?"

I shrugged. "Fine. No more frantic than usual. A few arguments with actors, here and there, but Kyle's a good boss. I'm lucky to have him around."

I expected Dr. Dillman would ask something about *us*, like how we've been getting along lately, or if there'd been any major changes in our professional lives, or if we spent quality time together, or if we made love often enough, or if we verbally communicated our needs, or if we shared responsibilities, but he was finished making inquiries.

He said, "I'd like to try something new." He laid his clipboard on the armrest and suggested that I might be better off taking Depakote, which is in a wholly different class of mood stabilizers. His guess was that I might have blood sugar complications, which would explain the adverse reaction I had to Risperdal. He said, "We ought to get you tested for diabetes."

You added, "He has been peeing a lot more, recently."

Dr. Dillman ignored you. He spoke at length about how Depakote regulates the stimulation and breakdown of a certain neurotransmitter. I didn't understand any of the science stuff, and didn't need to. All that mattered was his conclusion: Depakote has improved the quality of life for thousands of people.

You said, "So you think this is definitely chemical?"

He unfolded his legs. "Well, I can't say with absolute certainty—"

"Of course," you said.

"But given the—" he looked at the ceiling as he searched for the right word, "oddity of this occurrence, I can more or less say that it was probably due to, if you will, improper neurotransmitter management. My suggestion: we'll start out on the lowest dose of Depakote, and monitor him from there. I'd also like you to take a half milligram of clonazepam, as needed, when you're feeling stressed."

So that was it. We'd all agreed that the true culprit was pharmaceutical malfunction. The troubled look that you'd carried for days leaked away. I was off the hook, at least medically. But there were still wider social concerns that we needed to work through. First of which was our mutual deceit toward our loved ones.

On the night of the incident, after you'd stormed out of the apartment, took the Honda, and drove to Tara's house, I thought the police would come and seize me. But somewhere between our neighborhood and Tara's, you decided it'd be best to conceal the truth. You created a fiction about your injury, and

I would thereafter become complicit in propagating the story.

Tara had called me at around midnight. I trembled when the phone rang. "If you're looking for your wife, she's with me," Tara said. "I'm taking her to the hospital."

I gulped. I said nothing. Six or seven breaths later, Tara said, "You there?"

"I'm here."

"Are you going to ask me what happened?"

"Is that a leading question?"

"Wally!" she said. "If this is how you deal with crisis, you better talk to your shrink. I'll cut to the chase. Elizabeth's OK. While you were out, she was playing the piano and the key guard fell on her hand."

"It *fell*?"

"Yes, that's what I said."

"While I was gone?"

"Jesus Christ. Listen, you might want to come to University Hospital. She's got at least one or two broken fingers."

"It fell?"

"Just get your ass here, OK?" She hung up.

It was a trap. Social Services would intercept me in the lobby. Photographers for *The Cincinnati Enquirer* would snap my picture and stream it to all their online subscribers. *Assistant Manager of Court Street Theater Assaults Aspiring Physicist Wife.* The police would squirt mace in my eyes. They'd throw me in a cell at the Justice Center. Feminists would gather outside, waving hedge trimmers.

Leave, I thought. Drive north again. Just keep driving this time.

I drove south, to the hospital. When I entered the ER's waiting room, you produced a smile. "Hello, honey," you said.

My hands started to shake.

Tara stood. "Thank God you came. I can go home now." She turned to you. "No offense, Liz. I hate hospitals."

"I appreciate your help."

She hugged you, wished you well, patted my back, and left.

You wouldn't look at me.

My senses felt heightened, perhaps as a psychological diversion. I could hear the snack machine humming, the sickly moans of neglected elders, the squeaky wheelchairs inching slowly across the lobby. The woman on the other side of the waiting room smelled like mothballs. Everything—even the brown plastic seats bolted to the floor—shined with Lysol splendor. A television mounted on the wall aired a commercial for Civil War commemorative plates. One plate showed a flattened panoramic view of Gettysburg, General Meade's army charging up Culp's Hill. The scene was depicted in foggy impressionism because nobody wants to discover hyper-realistic depictions of sharp and bloodied bayonets beneath their mashed potatoes.

"I'm sorry, Elizabeth," I said.

You were concealing your hand. I could see the ice-pack's turquoise edge. "I don't want to talk about it," you said.

"Why? Why didn't you just—"

"Because you're going to get some help and it won't happen again and I know in my heart that I didn't marry a wife-beater. Now," you said, burying your hand deeper into your side, "let's move on."

Three hours later, the doctor handed you a black Sharpie, and you handed it to me. I wrote on your cast, "I love you, always. Wally."

Your father felt terrible. I remember him calling the day after the accident, while you were up at campus. He said, "I should have checked the piano's screws before I drove it out there. They probably wiggled loose during the drive. What was I thinking?"

"I'll tighten the screws," I said, "but don't blame yourself. Who knows how it really happened?" I shivered at my own words.

By the time the cast was removed, we'd acclimated to conducting ourselves as if nothing had ever happened. But I can't say that you didn't act differently. You started washing the dishes more often. You used less lighting in the apartment. You ironed your clothes, took up knitting, and conversed more with our neighbors. The piano, however, remained untouched. Kyle would never come over for a lesson again.

I changed, too, Elizabeth. Not for the better.

After having abused you, I began to wonder if it truly was an isolated incident. Did my grandmother let Marvin off the hook just as easily the first time he punched her in the eye? Did they convince themselves that the occurrence would not repeat itself?

I fear that if I don't go on this journey, I'm going to end up like my grandfather. I've never told you much about him because I worried that you might become suspicious of my bloodline, that you might make a scientific assumption that I'm biologically predisposed toward wrecking lives.

"Why now?" you're thinking. "Why have you held off this crisis for four years?"

I will tell you. But not now. I haven't even left Cincinnati yet.

I'm still at the bagel shop. The morning rush's first wave has dispersed. It's 7:45AM, and I gather that soon, another cluster of carb and coffee addicts will cram into the place. I'm on my third cup of Turkish Dark. Between the first and second cup, I had to go to the restroom. While I was in there, I found a religious pamphlet next to the sink. I took it back to my table.

The front cover says, "Does God love you? Maybe..." The inside says, "...Maybe Not." The words are set against a background of fire. There's an 800-number at the bottom of the page, along with some assurance, in case you thought you were fucked: "You Can Always Come Home To Your Father."

Prodigal Son allusions make me feel uncomfortable. The story sends an inaccurate message about human nature. Think about it: some kid runs away and blows his entire inheritance. He returns home when he's broke. The father, who represents God, greets his wayward son with open arms and forgives the irresponsible little shit. This is the same God who once declared, "I will reduce the wicked to heaps of rubble, along with the rest of humanity." The moral of the story is that everyone, including God, is inconsistent. A more realistic version would flash-forward to a year after the Prodigal Son's return, when everything *seemed* settled and just right. The father, who'd been biting his tongue for twelve months, who'd been secretly plotting revenge, would enter the kid's quarters in the middle of the night and drive a tent peg through the brat's knee so he'd never wander off again. "There, you son of a bitch!" the father would say. "Lesson learned."

You're probably envisioning a similar—though not as violent—narrative pertaining to the current state of our marriage. You're no doubt vacillating between wanting to forgive and wanting to murder. You're pissed because you didn't see this one coming. The last time I left, my departure had seemed inevitable. I'd been moping about the apartment for weeks, whining about being depressed, accusing the vapid world of belittling my aesthetic distinctiveness, of stomping out the already dying embers of my soul, of plundering my identity. "I need to find myself!" I'd said, again and again. You'd argued that my recent obsession was irrational: "Self? Self? That's so abstract, Wally. It's not like *the self* is a stable object, something you can locate and describe. It's a friggin' concept! It's elusive. You want to know who you are right now? I'll tell you. You're a guy who's obsessed with self-discovery. That's it. There's nothing to discover about that. And maybe next week, you'll be someone different." All this from the woman who searched relentlessly for the B-Gravitrope, which, back then, was only a concept.

Regardless of how ridiculous my pursuit was, I at least provided a motive for my departure. Now, I've given you nothing but a note taped to the shower curtain. I'm wary about explaining the full extent of my motives, which, unbeknownst to you, stretch back farther than Kyle and have their origins in my childhood. A few definitive sentences would be too much for you to process. You're in a state of panic, and therefore both incapable of producing an empathetic response and prone to misunderstanding my logic. Assuming that you read these letters in order—which I hope you do—you'll detect an ongoing change in my temperament as I ease you into an understanding. You'll notice my growing emotional resilience as I move along 3,962 miles of asphalt. In theory, this journey will enable me to radically de-victimize myself, and, consequently, you. I'll finally get over my past, which has, up until now, been the master of my emotions. I want to be ambivalent, like Peter Prynne; for all the crap that he went through, he didn't feel a goddamn thing.

You roll your eyes. You're not interested in "a 350-year-old misogynist!"

Unless you learn to appreciate Peter Prynne and what he's meant to my family, you'll never understand why I'm always compelled to leave. I'm not giving you a choice anymore. You want healthy marital communications? Then, for once, stop impeding me from telling you Peter's story.

Besides, I know the real reason why you obstruct my narrative. You've read my journals. You think I'm nuts for admiring Peter so much. It makes you jealous.

Here's your chance to begin to grow in understanding of your husband. Here's why I hold Peter Prynne in the highest regards.

As far as I can recall, you know that Peter was a Royalist in the English Civil War, and that he was arrested in 1644 and hanged the next day. You know that he survived because the rope snapped. But your knowledge stops about there, correct?

Here's what happened next, whether you like it or not. On the night that the rope snapped, Royalist spies smuggled him out of prison and hid him in a Catholic church's basement. He stayed there for two years. What Peter did during that time is arguable because his journals were seized and—according to Aunt Martha—they were burned. But we do know that Peter's former friend, a playwright named Jonathan Valve, snitched. He gave Prynne's whereabouts. Valve's famous words were, "I have Peter Prynne! I have Peter Prynne!" When Peter was dragged to the gallows a second time, the crowd repeated Valve's declaration, "I have Peter Prynne!" Imagine what that was like for Peter! To be betrayed by a playwright—that speaks volumes to me. Especially since Kyle is, apparently, a playwright, and he's constantly trying to get you in bed.

The Parliamentarians tried to hang Peter again. Instead of his neck snapping, the rope broke again. After a failed third attempt, they simply stabbed Peter in the stomach, and hanged the man who couldn't tie a proper knot.

Three unsuccessful efforts to hang a man! What does that say about resilience? Peter knew how to hold his head up high, so high that it could rip through an inch of tightly twisted hemp.

Also, Peter Prynne wasn't just physically uncompromising. His emotional indifference was beautiful:

June 8, 1635
Today young Miranda cuckolded me with an older gentleman from the theater. Then I tended to the orchards where the apples were ripe. I saw three kinds of birds and six deer. The sky was mildly dull.

Miranda is mentioned extensively throughout the years 1634-35 because Peter was pursuing her. After his one, passionless reference to cuckolding, he never discussed her again. This leads me to believe that Peter saw love as a petty affliction. By contrast, after Parliament's revolt against King Charles, Peter wrote long-winded oaths about divine right and a unified church. His bland musings favored reason over the instability of emotion. I want to be like that, Elizabeth.

I bet you're wondering what our relationship would be like if I became as impervious as Peter Prynne. "I'd be better off married to a cinderblock," you're thinking.

You already are. You've complained about how I'm emotionally constipated, how the energy I'd otherwise use to appreciate you gets channeled into all sorts of ludicrous projects, like playing in cover bands with 40-year-old burnouts and writing one-act plays that aren't even good enough for Amateur Appreciation Night at the most backcountry community theaters. This road trip will teach me to become resilient toward everything but you. If I can shrink my perceived radius of psychological burdens, invalidate its enormity, depreciate its affective potency, then the bed we share—by virtue of comparison—will become bigger and bigger. This kind of abandonment, it's an act of necessity rather than selfishness. You'll eventually reap the rewards.

Christ, I've just explained myself. I didn't want to do that. But I'm not about to crumple up these last few pages and throw them in the trash. It's not the whole story anyway. I'd be a fool to envision you nodding your head and saying, "Oh, I get it. This makes perfect sense." You're probably checking the medicine cabinet. You're counting the pills in your palm and coming to the realization that I haven't been taking them. That explains it all, right? Wally's having delusions.

That's what you thought last time as I drove on toward Inuvik, hoping to unlearn everything that I thought was true about life. But I only made it as far as Wisconsin. You called me on the cell phone, crying. You said, "Have you been taking your medicine, Wally? See! See! This is what happens when you stop taking your medicine! Please, come home!"

One end of the rope was in Cincinnati, and the other around my neck, its grip becoming tighter the further north I drove. I turned the car around, afraid of consequences.

The crazy thing was that I had been taking my meds. I hadn't missed a day. When I got home, I lied. I said, "I'm so sorry, Liz... I wanted to see if I could live without being dependent on pharmaceutical companies. I understand the dangers now." One lie and we could just put everything behind us. That's our pattern, isn't it?

Things have changed. Last night, while you were asleep, I stashed my bags in the car. I felt no hesitancy because I kept in mind that Peter Prynne didn't believe in consequences. Regardless of the improbability of surviving, he was determined to arrive intact at his destination—the ground.

This time, I'm through with medication. I'm going all-natural and utilizing the most effective therapeutic mediums: experience and distance. Trust me, Elizabeth, although you may feel wounded right now, this is going to work.

It's time to leave for Inuvik, 4,000 miles from here.

———————

I'm in a traffic jam and writing on a notepad while the car idles. The twelve-mile hold-up is the result of roadwork, but I have yet to see a construction team. Instead, I see rows of deceitful flashing signs that say, "Construction Ahead." We drivers should band together and sue the Highway Department for malpractice. But instead, we do what's natural when our expectations aren't being met: we freeze. My only means of distraction is to continually note the similarity between commuters' expressions and drought-dried farmlands. However, there is one constituent to this vapid landscape that challenges uniformity. Every few miles, I've passed miniature oil drills. They're called pumpjacks. Their rhythmic stroking motions fascinate me. I liken it to a mechanical finger-fucking of the earth. Plus, their nose-down nose-up oscillations are compensating for our lack of movement.

Speaking of dormancy, I should mention this: Have you noticed how our married life had been excruciatingly inactive until you published that paper on dark matter rotational curves? Do I even have the topic right? We never took the time to explain things like gravitational physics and Peter Prynne to each other.

When I look back at the four years leading up to your publication and breakthrough discovery of the B-Gravitrope, I see on the surface a couple who'd grown bored with one another. Whereas we once spent hours sitting on the couch, riffing beautifully off each other's thoughts, ideas, and opinions about philosophy and science and art, our conversations now look like this:

You: Can you please pass the salt?

Me: I can't reach it from here. Use the serving spoon to pull the shaker toward you.

You: It's dripping with soup. Why don't you just get up?

Me: Because I'm sitting.

You: Fine. Then I'll get up.

Then, silence for the rest of the meal. In fact, silence for the rest of the evening, until you say, "I'm going to bed," and then I say, "Goodnight."

We certainly acted like a bored couple. We weren't jaded, though. We were selfish and lazy. Maybe even scared. We broke our problems down into three categories: yours, mine, and occasionally, ours. Can you see the quandary here? Yes, we are accountable for our own shortcomings, but to compartmentalize our difficulties, to keep them private, whether out of shame or to "protect" each other, only obstructs our ability to communicate.

As the division between us grew, we started doing all sorts of harmful things to compensate. For instance, instead of coming to me to fulfill your interpersonal needs, you channeled your enthusiasm into Kyle. I won't let myself off the hook here; I avoided you by frequently retreating to my office, where I wrote one dumb play after another. I joined a bar band full of men who were avoiding their wives, too.

Now that I've diagnosed the problem, here's there solution: we develop an active interest in each other's passions. Even if we have to fake it for a while, I've no doubt that sincerity emerges out of willingness. But we have to be patient, too. Six months ago, when you finally discovered the B-Gravitrope, I tried to read up on physics. You were rather hostile about the sources I'd chosen: all Barnes & Noble books. So I gave up on trying to comprehend the most important achievement in your life. Now, for the sake of our marriage, I'm redoubling my efforts. Hell, I've already taken some initiative. I read a third of your article last night. Granted, I don't understand it, but I'm excited about one thing: the subtext. Every phrase, formula, and idea you've written indirectly conveys a sense of departure, as if, somewhere deep inside, you know that traveling beyond our comforts, literally, is necessary if we want to make progress.

You've inspired me to adopt a similar methodology, however different our circumstances. You look for ways to evade gravity and I must succumb to it. Whereas you'll soon travel the continents, giving lectures on gravitomagnetic fields, I cannot claim that the cultivation of minds propels my motion. Yet, we're both searching for *the answer*, and we both know that in order to find it, we must leave home.

Elizabeth, we've neglected each other's intellects over the years, and it's pulled us apart. I've already taken some steps to understand physics, and I'm now asking you to make an effort to understand me. Unfortunately, I haven't provided you all of the necessary information to form an accurate profile of your husband —I've kept my childhood a secret all these years.

————————

I'm writing you from a booth at a Denny's. The "No Smoking" sign on the wall is making me want a cigarette. This Nicorette doesn't do shit. I've got four pieces in my mouth right now, and I'm waiting for the serotonin buzz that I'd otherwise get from a Marlboro. It hasn't come yet. Giving Nicorette to a nicotine addict is like giving Tic Tacs to a heroin junky.

I got off at the nearest exit because of the traffic. Half the motorists on the highway did the same thing, and the Denny's parking lot was full of idling cars. People had their seats reclined and air conditioner vents pointed at their faces. One woman, sitting on the hood of her Ford truck, was breastfeeding her baby. She nodded as I passed her. I swear that the baby nodded, too—I mean, that's what I saw. He turned around, inclined his little head, and looked right at me. It was more of a resigned shrug than a nod, like he was saying, "Hey, I know this is socially awkward, you can see my mom's tits and all, but it's not like there's much else to do out here." He went back to sipping his mother's nipple, and I wondered if my sleep deprivation was catching up to me.

I walked into the restaurant's foyer. A speaker in the ceiling played Weather Channel music, and the place smelled like grease and old people.

I slipped two quarters into the payphone, and dialed the 800-number that was on the damnation-themed pamphlet I'd found in the bagel shop's restroom earlier this morning. I felt deprived of human interaction. My dispute with Kyle hardly counted.

After three rings, a woman on the other line said, "Divine intervention hotline. This is Becky. Can I help you?"

I said, "Hello. My name is Wally. I read your brochure this morning. I want to know if it's true, if God really loves me."

She said, "Give me a second here, Wally, while I get my Bible." I could hear her lips pulling back into a smile. "OK, in the book of Jeremiah it says, 'The Lord has appeared of old to me, saying, Yes, I have loved you with an everlasting love. Therefore with loving kindness I have drawn you.'"

She paused a moment. "Wally, the Lord has drawn you to me. It's no coincidence that you're calling. It doesn't matter whether you're an adulterer, a homosexual, a lesbian, a fornicator, whatever. All you need to do is to accept the invitation into the Lord's house. The invitation is written in the blood of his only Son, Jesus Christ. Is that not love, Wally?"

"It's love," I said. An elderly couple, both with walkers, struggled to open the restaurant's front doors. I reached and pulled the door's handle. Warm air from outside blew in. The old man was wearing a Korean War Veterans hat. Their walkers knocked the floor as they passed me.

I said to Becky, "I want to meet God."

"You will, when it's time to be judged."

"I want to meet him sooner than that."

"He's already working in your life, Wally. Otherwise, you never would have called me."

"Right," I said. "I just wanted to make sure. I guess I should get going now."

She replied quickly. No doubt, she was trying to keep me on the phone. "Where are you going?" she said.

"North. I'm running away from my life." The word north made me think of Santa Claus. My imagination lit up with an image that I had entertained when I was a child. I saw Santa perched atop a tower that was affixed to his North Pole toy factory, the snow gently descending from the night sky. He was looking through a telescope and spinning the focus wheel so that he could scrutinize in detail my every sin.

My stomach knotted. I felt all the raw emotion that I had long ago associated with Christmas: an obsessive determination to be good, the subsequent guilt because I always fell short of Santa's ridiculous ideals and, ultimately, humiliation because Santa had validated his unfavorable opinion of me.

Becky said, "Why are you running away from your life?"

"I'll tell you some other time," I said. "I have a more pressing concern at the moment. I'd like to ask you another question."

"I'll answer anything. I've got my Bible right here."

"Are Christians supposed to be telling their children that there's a Santa Claus?"

I heard pages flipping in the background. She said, "Santa Claus isn't real. It's a lie, and Paul tells us in Colossians, 'Lie not one to another.' Also, Santa's a false God. Children can't make the distinction, and that's bad."

Exactly, I thought. She continued, "You want to know something else? Santa says, 'Ho ho ho,' right? Guess where he got that from?"

"Paul?" I said.

"No, but good guess. In Zechariah 2, God says, 'Ho, ho, come forth, and flee from the land of the north.'"

I said, "Hmm. Odd. I'm going north."

"I know! And ho, ho, God is telling you that you shouldn't. Otherwise, I would never have thought to quote that specific passage. The Holy Spirit inspired me."

"Amazing," I said. "But I'm still going."

She was quiet for a second. I heard her sip something, perhaps a cup of tea. But I wouldn't be surprised if it was a martini. "Wally, if you really want God's guidance, then you're probably going to have to be a little more specific with me. What's going on, exactly?"

I said, "I don't feel like I'm in a place where I can make that kind of confession. Maybe I'll call you again tomorrow."

"I hope you do. The Lord handpicked you, Wally."

"That makes me feel special."

"It should."

"I'll call you tomorrow, Becky."

"Please, do. It sounds like you really need help. May the Lord bless you."

And that was it. God loves me.

What I should have asked was, "Why does God allow horrible people to exist?"

Becky would have said, "Humans have free will. It's not God's fault."

I would have asked her why God permits free will. This is a sophomoric argument, but I'm getting at something here, Elizabeth. This has to do with family history.

I'm not the first person in my family who's used travel as a means to elicit personal growth. My crazy granduncle Don Donovan—another name you refuse to acknowledge— frequently left his wife and kids. He'd hop a train and go wherever it brought him, more often than not to places where he could gamble the family's finances away. When he was forty years old, he took one final journey. He went north, as far as he could go, and ended up in Inuvik. Nobody knows what happened to him while he was there, but when he came back he was sober and sane. He got a real job, and treated his wife well until the day he died.

Remember how, when I first started submitting my dramas to theatrical producers, I used his last name rather than my own? I called myself Wally Donovan. It had a bounce to it, like the gait of an unemployed symphony conductor. I reasoned that my own last name, Tiparoy, sounded synonymous with "small pecker." In truth, my decision had nothing to do with branding myself. I was trying to linguistically embody Uncle Donovan's propensity to change. You might have read about this in my diary. Certainly, I have no proof that you've invaded my privacy, that you've flipped through page after page, bawling, reading about my sexual fantasies, my genealogical obsessions—but still, why else would you shriek whenever I mentioned my relatives?

Four years ago, following the key-guard incident, I admitted that my ideal sense of self—modeled around Peter Prynne and Don Donovan—had failed to materialize. If I ever wanted to become a better person, I'd need to do more than adopt a new name. So I made my first attempt at a therapeutic road trip to Inuvik. That's what I meant about finding myself. The impetus for my journey was based on my assumption that I had inherited at least some favorable traits—like Peter and Don's—from my mother's side of the family, but those genes were latent, in need of activation. The genes that had currently monopolized my attitudes and behaviors were more indicative of my father's side of the family: moody, emotional, never satisfied, and prone to depression. Although my father had succeeded in overcoming his disposition, I lacked his discipline and strength to act contrary to nature. My only hope, it seemed, was to incite my mother's dormant genes via a transformative experience.

As you know, my trip was cut short. I don't blame you for that. You did what any concerned wife would do: you called your missing husband's cell phone. I'd set myself up by bringing the phone with me. Clearly, I wasn't ready for the journey. This time, however, I feel like I've got a chance. I've left all technology behind. Hell, I've already made a lot of introspective progress.

Earlier today, while driving, I searched my memories for the earliest indication that I'd live a life of never-ending dissatisfaction. What had been the catalyst? Was it the first time my parents left me alone in my bedroom? A particular thunderstorm that scared me? The day when my parents announced they'd be spending an indefinite amount of time volunteering in China? The first time that Marvin was violent toward me?

I passed a Toys "R" Us and immediately reminisced on the toys that I *hadn't* received in my childhood; specifically, a Transformers action figure that I didn't get in 1983, one called Soundwave. That year, Santa had broken his mythological contract: I'd been a good first-grader, a good grandson, I'd made a list, and he delivered useless, dollar-store garbage. There it was—the initial conditions of my unhappiness.

Soundwave was the least functional Transformer. While his cohorts morphed into practical things like jets and trucks, he changed into a stationary household item. Through a series of simple maneuvers, the robot became a cassette player. Soundwave's inability to play actual cassettes further exemplified his uselessness. His only noteworthy feature was an eject button that opened the cassette door, and two cannons that were shaped like AA batteries. The cassette tray was situated on his chest when he stood in full, biped robot posture. I wanted it. His inadequacy made him all the more desirable.

More importantly, though, my childish mind associated the hope of receiving the toy with the hope of my parents returning home from missionary work in China. They'd already been gone over two years, and had left my sister and me in Marvin and Aunt Eve's care. What I didn't know—and what nobody knew other than Marvin, Eve, and our parish's priest—was that authorities in China had placed my parents in prison. I take that back. "Prison" isn't quite the word. They'd been detained for supporting anti-government activities and placed in a minimum-security work camp. Their frequent letters home, specifically the ones addressed to Molly and me, were devoid of any indication that they'd been arrested. As far as I knew, they were running around the streets converting people.

That summer, I'd discovered Soundwave. In a letter to my parents, I described the toy. They replied, "Soundwave sounds amazing! We're hoping to be back this Christmas, so don't go spend your allowance on Soundwave, hint hint. We want to be there when Santa delivers it. In case we don't get home by Thanksgiving, tell Grandpa to help you make a Christmas list. Make sure you put Soundwave on it!"

By Christmas, my parents were still gone. Every letter they sent said, "Just a few more months." This went on for years.

My sister got a real cassette player that Christmas. She would record Boy George and Cindy Lauper songs off the radio. I was terribly jealous because I got three different colored footballs. They were red, white, and blue. I subverted their intended functions, drew windows on them, and transformed them into spaceships.

Had my parents been at home, I would have asked them to assist me in writing a letter to Santa, requesting Soundwave. Their version of my Christmas list would have been more effective than the ones Marvin helped me write. I recall it now, Elizabeth. Marvin hovered behind me as I sat at the kitchen table, his greasy sweat like doughnut glaze, his heavy panting a constant flux of bad breath that rippled my hair. I steadied my pencil on the paper and wrote: *Dear Santa Clause—*

"No!" Marvin screamed. "What the hell are they teachin' you in school? Get rid of the E at the end."

I went on: *This Christmas I want—*

"Not yet!" Marvin yelled. "Did you write him a thank-you card last winter?"

"Uh, no."

He put his hand on my shoulder and squeezed, as if crushing an orange. "Then you need to apologize."

I ignored the pain and tried to write: *Dear Santa Claus, I'm sorry I didn't send you a card last year. Thank you for the toys. This yea—*

Marvin tightened his grip so hard his knuckles popped. I didn't flinch or protest for fear that he'd seize my other shoulder. He said, "Have your parents ever taught you about humility, or do they think you'll do just fine without it, like your dad?"

"I don't know," I said. The tears I held back burned.

"Well, you're going to learn. First off, if you were sorry for not sending a card, you wouldn't need me to tell you that, would you? You'd just know it. So quit being a fucking liar."

I wrote: *Dear Santa Claus. I'm sorry that I wasn't sorry for not sending a card.*

I glanced at Marvin for approval. His eyes looked like the surface of a black lake. He wanted to drown me, fill my lungs with stagnant water until I choked. "And?" he said.

"And what?"

"And tell him you've been inconsiderate about the amount of work that he does."

He helped me with the spelling, word after word: *I'm sorry that I wasn't sorry for not sending a card. I've been inconsiderate about the amount of work you do.*

Marvin dictated what came next. *I probably don't deserve anything for being a selfish brat who always believes that things should go my own way. Give my toys to the kid who needs them, who worked for them.*

I turned to Marvin. "I'm not really like that."

He said, "Oh, you are. Now write this down: I never clean my room or mow the lawn or shovel snow. Instead, I waste time watching TV. If you're going to get me anything, get me a set of tools, some backbone, and an alarm clock that goes off at 6AM. If I don't change my ways, then bring me a tampon so that I can shove it up my little ass."

I looked down at what I had written. "I'm not sending this," I said.

"Like hell you aren't," he said, snatching the letter from the table. "I am."

I tried to grab it from him, but he stuck out his palm. I leapt, my fingers spread long and wide, but he lifted the letter over his head. Tears broke from my eyes. "You're not sending it!" I cried, "I want Soundwave!"

"You don't deserve it."

"That's not what Mom and Dad think!"

He laughed. "Really? Really? You believe those letters they send? They just don't want to break your heart. The fact is they don't ever think about you. You're the last thing on their minds, and always have been. If they actually cared about you, they wouldn't be in China, would they?"

I jumped at the letter again, and this time he blocked me with his leg.

All I could do was collapse into the chair. He stomped out of the kitchen, yelling to whoever was in the house, "Where're the stamps? Anthony's kid is gonna learn a valuable lesson this Christmas."

Marvin was right. I did learn a valuable lesson. I discovered that no matter what, I would be unhappy.

Six months ago, when you discovered the B-Gravitrope, I knew things were going to change. I wanted to know what it meant to "discover" a particle, if it was a big deal or an ordinary occurrence in the physics world. According to some of the consumer-friendly physics books I purchased, there's a hazy area between finding a new particle and being responsible for its creation. One book suggests the neutron didn't exist until someone looked for it. Somehow, in the quantum world, mind and matter are linked. You've warned me about these absurdities, but I don't have the intellectual capacity to discern true science from New Age hogwash. In any case, I learned that scientists are discovering particles all the time. Most of them are junk, their existences so brief that they're labeled "virtual." I felt somewhat relieved because if you became famous, we might face more marital problems. Low and behold, my worries had merit. Elizabeth, when you brought that particle to life, you changed our marriage. You became something, and I lingered in nothingness.

———————

Now that I'm interested in physics, I have a million questions that I'd like you to answer. I plan on asking them, too. Here's one: is reality fixed, or elastic like space-time? I'm not asking about events that occur within reality, but reality itself. Please don't tell me that reality is the events that occur within it.

One of those pop-science books I read, *Quantum Miracles*, says that at a subatomic level, past, present, and future exist simultaneously. Particles don't operate in "human time." Every interaction they've ever had is "functionally embedded" in the present because the past never dissipates. If this stuff is true, are you taken aback by its metaphorical significance? Do you even understand what I'm saying? If the building blocks of all matter in the universe are impervious to time—if their present states are also their past and future states—then what does that say about the human mind? To me, it means that at the material core of my being, the past and future exist simultaneously, but my consciousness—like everyone else's—insists on creating and perceiving an illusionary, incremental progression of events. Why? Because if I recognized that the past continues to happen—to be ever-present—I'd be more fucked up than I already am. I would suffer through my childhood traumas indefinitely. Yes, it's beneficial that our minds compartmentalize time, but there are always drawbacks. We're detached from the intrinsic structure of reality. We spend our lives trying to let go of the past because, according to psychologists and self-help books, it's the healthy thing to do. In truth, we're committing ourselves to an impossible task;

in order to genuinely kiss our erstwhile pains goodbye, we must also purge ourselves of the present, because they're one and the same. No wonder why trauma victims stay crazy. The only way out, it seems, is to kill yourself.

Here I am, on a road trip that's supposed to enlighten me, to help me get over my past and become a "whole" person, the kind of man that you've always wanted me to be, and I'm beginning to suspect that I'm bound to fail—that in some cases, change is just impossible. You probably felt that way when you set out to find the B-Gravitrope. I don't know. I never asked.

———

Like you, my sister has been fortunate in her field, microbiology. She discovered a fungus, one that had been hypothetical for a long time, one that has special properties that are now widely used in tuberculosis treatments. I've discovered a fungus, too. It's the inherited transgressions of Grandpa Marvin. It's his genes superimposed on my own, his past embedded in my present.

We've barely spoken about my family, but for Peter Prynne. Whenever you've asked about my family, I've said, "Let's not go there." You assumed that I was talking about the car crash that took my parents away from the earth. I wasn't. I was talking about Grandpa.

———

I've ordered blueberry pancakes. They're cold and terrible. The kitchen is backed up due to all the people fleeing the highway and I doubt I'll get a chance to order anything else. The elderly couple with the walkers are sitting in the booth behind me.

I've just overheard their conversation. The old man said to his wife, "Your brother is a shit head. After all these years, still a shit head."

She paused, then said, "I'm sorry."

His coffee mug clanked against the saucer. "It's not your fault."

"I know."

He said, "Is this the smoking section?"

"I don't think so."

"Fuck."

They were quiet again. I pressed my cheap plastic fork into my cheap plastic pancake and waited to hear if they had anything else to say to each other.

He's an old man. His skin is olive colored. He either spends a lot of time on his front porch, or he owns a beach house in Florida. He hasn't shaved the back of his neck and shoulders in ages. He reminds me of Grandpa Marvin. They look similar, and they cuss the same way. Their voices rise an octave when they say dirty words.

If I failed to demonstrate this, I'll say it again: Marvin was a horrible human being. Because of him, my father didn't have a childhood. Grandpa forced him to work six days a week on a dump truck. Dad didn't get to play ball with his friends because he was laboring well into the evening, loading the stinky truck with TV dinners, newspapers, and soiled furniture, while Marvin sat in the driver's seat, chain-smoking and drinking. On Saturdays, Marvin would rip Dad out of bed before sunrise and force him into the truck. Dad would come home dirty, dripping with sweat and diaper piss and sticky soda sap and ketchup. He'd have a gloomy face, and Marvin, having consumed the equivalent of three fish-tanks of beer and vodka, would say, "Change your face or I'll do it for you."

My father tried throughout his life to compensate for his missing childhood. He gambled, drank, boxed, and raced cars. Naturally, he hated his father, and no amount of prayer or psychotherapy could eradicate the son of a bitch from Dad's mind. The only reasonable thing he could do was help other people. That's why he became a fireman. And that's how he overcame his inherited vices: he discovered that by helping others, he was helping himself.

Thirty minutes ago, the Denny's waitress gave me my check. Now she's flicking annoyed glances at me. I suppose her shift's ended and she wants her tip. I'd like to get moving too, but I feel overwhelmingly inert. I know what the problem is: my unconscious mind is trying to protect the status quo. It sees the discomforting correlation between introspection and driving. It's telling me to remain immobile. After all, who really wants to mine all their frightening memories? I've barely started, and it's already been somewhat harrowing. Nonetheless, I best get moving before I convince myself to go back home.

After sitting still for an hour on the highway, I turned around. State route 27 took me north, a little out of the way, but then I took the Ross Mountain bypass back to 74.

You knew I'd screw that one up, didn't you? You were thinking, "He's going to get lost. He's terrible with directions." Indeed, I ended up on Interstate 70, and this whole mess cost me three and a half hours. But I was finally out of Ohio and into Indiana.

This is where America flattens out, as if long ago the Midwest was as an ironing board for God's lab coat. The people out here know the geography has lost its cosmic functionality, but they don't understand why. Now, they have no shame. Men wear oversized John Deere hats and sport mullets. They fill their cheeks with snuff and spit at everything. The air is humid and stinking of pig entrails.

While stopping to get coffee at a gas station, I talked to the woman behind the cash register. I wanted some human interaction. Her name was Kelly. She was a college student, and her summer job was at the BP. "What's your field of study?" I said.

Her cheeks became rosy. "Environmental Sciences."

"How's our environment?"

She was fidgety, like a windup toy with a broken gear. She said, "It's not as bad as people say. What about you? What are you up to today?"

"I'm nervous."

"Hmm," she said. "Some kind of business thing? You look like you're on business." The register flashed $1.09.

I dug through my wallet. "Nah, nothing like that. I'm driving four thousand miles north to the Yukon."

"A delivery?"

"No. A deliverance." I slid the money toward her. "I've left my wife, and now I'm going north to blame Santa Claus for fucking up my childhood."

Her eyes flashed like an internal warning system. She shuffled the money into the register. "Do you want a receipt?"

"I'm good."

I said one more thing before leaving. "Hey, did Santa always give you what you wanted?"

She thought for a second, her hands pressed on the counter firmly. "I think so. Even if he didn't, it was no big deal because I enjoyed everything I got."

"You're not like me," I said. The door chimed as I left. I got back in the Honda and drove until sundown.

Tonight, I camp at Devil's Lake, Wisconsin. The first time I ran away from you, this was about as far as I'd gotten. I don't feel as constricted this time because I know every mile from here on will purge me of my guilt complex, my pessimism, my failure to interact with the people I love, my genetic predisposition, and, most importantly, my need to take medicine. My brain will naturally reconstruct itself, and you'll be happy that I've changed.

Right now, your soul feels calloused. Your eyes are sore from tears. Every time you think of me, it's like a hundred insect bites. I assure you, sooner or later, you'll realize that my decision to leave made perfect sense. You'll be so glad that you married me. Just continue to read these letters, in order, and it'll all come together.

The rangers gave me site number 137 because I'd arrived late. It's at the northeast corner of the campground, a good distance from the lake. From this far out, among the birches and pines, you'd expect the place to be as peaceful as a Rembrandt landscape. Not quite. All the late-comers and derelicts have been grouped together. It's 9PM, and people are erecting their tents, situating satellites on top of their RVs in order to get the best signal for summer reruns. Twilight is here, the sky's edge glowing red like a kiln. The crickets are thunderous, hypnotizing, a steady drone against the warm upward waves of wind in the trees. The maple leaves look like brooms, swooshing the air back and forth. Camping makes me feel like a child cradled in my mother's arms, nurtured in the woods' reassuring lie that everything will be all right. I can smell the combination of wood and newspapers burning in fire pits, hear the dogs barking, their owners hushing them. I was foolish not to bring a tent, but having never slept beneath the stars, I thought I'd maybe see the northern lights.

Firewood is expensive. I'd originally made a campfire out of park brochures, the *New York Times*, a few twigs, and insect repellant, but it was reduced to ashes in less than two minutes. I considered burning one of the books I'd brought along: Bertrand Russell's *Why I'm Not a Christian*. I've made several attempts to read the book, but so far, I haven't gotten past the first chapter. Knowing that I'd regret setting a book ablaze, I bought a $9.00 bundle of wood. The first two logs burned so fast they might as well have been cardboard. I threw in two more logs. Within seconds, the orange embers on the bottom ignited them, discharging golden flames, which quickly diminished and let out a purr. I need more park brochures.

Everyone is inside their RVs, watching sitcoms, blue light flickering through their blinds. A few moments ago, an RV door opened and two children stepped outside. A mother in a yellow nightgown stood there barefoot and said, "You can come back in an hour. No sooner. Daddy and I are watching porno movies."

Those kids are going to be screwy when they grow up. One will be a pimp and the other a pole dancer. The parents probably came from deranged families as well. I want to know. Had I fewer inhibitions, I'd knock on their RV door in an hour and request an interview. I'd tell them I'm a reporter for *American Family Magazine* and that I'm doing an article on ancestry. But right now, I shouldn't be thinking about investigating other people's family histories, not when I have yet to tell you my own.

Here's some more lineage for you. I might have tried to explain this on our honeymoon, but I recall that you had more important things in mind. The first historical account of Peter Prynne dates back to 1579 in reference to his father's execution. Michael Prynne was a traveling actor who did not have a patron. His lack of sponsorship was in direct violation to Queen Elizabeth's law prohibiting vagrancy and wandering. He'd gotten in trouble for this six times already, so when Michael was arrested for the seventh time, they took him to the rack. First, they clipped off his genitals. Then they opened him up, stuffed three live rats in his gut, and sewed him back shut.

Michael Prynne was not so resilient, according to Peter's journal: *My father shrieked as the rats gnawed his spleen. He turned toward me, saw the tears running from my eyes, and he quoted Marlowe, 'O soul, be changed into little water drops, and fall into the ocean, ne'er be found.' I could not tell if he was speaking to me or to God. But I swore, after this day, I would never cry again.*

Peter was adopted by his uncle Henry, an apple orchard owner. After Henry's death, Peter inherited the orchard, and was a farmer for twenty years. He had many wives and children in many places. Then, one day, the government seized the orchard. The trees were cut down and used for building warships. He'd never been politically active before, but this unwarranted seizure of land became the prime instigator for his future alliances.

One of Peter Prynne's many daughters married John Donovan, an Irish clockmaker. Hence came the Donovans, branching out sixteen generations. My grandmother, Lucy Donovan, married an engineer named Jim Southpaw. Lucy and Jim had my mother, Carla.

In 1968, Carla Southpaw met my father, Anthony Tiparoy, at a psychedelic rock club in New Jersey. They were waiting on line to use the bathroom and, coincidentally, my mother had in her purse the first-edition publication of Peter Prynne's journal. Everyone in her family got a copy.

She wanted to meet a gentleman that night, someone she could marry. She would use Prynne's journal to gauge her prospects, for she believed that a man who cannot appreciate a woman's history is a man who cannot endure a woman's presence. She encountered that special man on line while they both held their bowels. Standing beneath strobe lights and bombarded with earsplitting music, Carla handed Anthony the journal and he glanced at an entry in the middle of the book.

Now, I must consult my copy of Prynne's diaries. I've earmarked the page that I imagine led to my parents' inevitable union:

August 6, 1598

We wanted to see the kingdoms tolerate the Protestants. I am growing intolerable. I went to the new theater called Globes. The comedy was called Much Ado of This or That. I have seen this Shaksper before, it was a contrived folly, a waste of my afternoon. I will attend to Jonson's dramas for now on.

Anthony handed it back. He commented on Prynne's reference to the aftermath of the French wars, and also stated that Ben Jonson is an under-appreciated playwright. Carla found Anthony's intelligence impressive. But what sealed the deal was this: Anthony said, "This journal looks very, very interesting. Where can I get one?"

Carla put Prynne's journal back in Anthony's hands. She told him it was a loan; he'd have to return the book in a week, and also take her out for dinner.

Five years later, Carla gave birth to Molly, and three years after that, to me.

Although I would have preferred to inherit the Prynne-Donovan-Southpaw genes, I ended up with Marvin's. I've tried to outsmart my design with psychoanalysis, pills, pot, religion, denial, and determination, all to no avail. So maybe, when I reach the Yukon, my more destructive genes will freeze. Maybe abstract concepts like predisposition will become negligible in the extreme temperature. In the wintry sluggishness, my genes will have no other option but to be apathetic because the amount of energy needed to sustain my temperament won't be compatible with the Yukon environment.

In 1976, the year I was born, Grandpa Marvin had an epiphany. He was sixty-two and suffering cirrhosis of the liver. His wife had finally mustered the nerve to say, "You've been giving me black eyes since I was twenty-three. I can barely see anymore. I'm leaving you." She divorced him. Marvin couldn't survive on his own. Grandma had done his laundry and cooked his meals and folded his clothes and cleaned the tubs, toilets, and sinks; and now, alone, Marvin just stared at the appliances. His daughter Eve moved in with him and became his caretaker. He stopped drinking for the first time in forty years. He went to AA. It was a miracle.

The ninth step of AA involves making amends. One afternoon, Marvin came to our home. I was only a few years old, but I remember the emotional resonance. He sat at the kitchen table with Dad, who nervously bounced me on his knee. Dad wanted to tell him to just die in a fire, but perhaps he saw the unusual sincerity in Marvin's eyes. Dad needed real amends, though; not verbal promises and admissions of guilt, but a change of actions and behaviors. So Marvin wasn't forgiven right away. Over the next two years, Marvin became a regular participant in our family life. He took us out to eat twice a week, despite the lingering pain in his liver. He helped my parents buy a new home in Nanuet. Doubled over and sometimes retching, he did the yard work, though nobody had asked him to. He taught himself to cook and scrub the bathtub and fold laundry. He did it all for us, despite the resentment my father clung to. After those two years, it was safe to say that Marvin had made living amends. One afternoon, I overheard them in the kitchen. Dad was making coffee, and Grandpa was washing the dishes. Dad whispered, "I'm proud of you."

I don't know if Dad embraced him, or if Grandpa continued to wash the dishes while Dad scooped coffee beans, but I felt the psychic atmosphere change. He was now a part of the family after a long, long hiatus.

And it was then, Elizabeth, that my dark period began.

Tonight I will sleep under the stars on our memory foam. I realized that I wouldn't be able to sleep without it. The other night, right before I left, I used a box cutter to sever the foam right down the center. You didn't stir, despite your recent restlessness. You were drained from having spent the early part of the evening throwing up those awful burritos I'd made.

Remember how we argued about whether or not we should buy the memory foam? First, I complained, "What, our king-sized bed isn't comfortable enough for you?" Then I bitched about money. But the moment I laid down on the one-inch thick mattress, I agreed with you, and tonight I want to feel the same as I did then. I deserve a good night's sleep.

July 28

It's morning now. Everyone else is asleep. It's quiet—your kind of "back to nature" serenity. The air is fresh, and dew sparkles on all the leaves. Shafts of sunlight shine through the tree branches, intersecting in a vast, golden cobweb. I can see the lake from my campsite if I stand on top of a rock. It's like an iridescent silver coin bashed into the ground. When I stand, I see the sky's blue reflection on the water. When I sit, I see the inverted image of green trees. Had I not known any better, I'd be under the illusion that my positioning can change the properties of the lake's surface.

I want to stop in St. Paul and find the mega-church where the famous evangelical theologian Greg Boyd preaches. He's one of the few who don't irritate me. I used to listen to his sermons as downloaded mp3s when I was a practicing Christian. As it turned out, I'd been practicing for the day I'd leave the Christian community. Back then—this was about a month after I'd slammed the key guard on your fingers—I was desperate for anything that would make me into someone other than myself. I thought that Jesus might be the answer. And it seemed like he was, until his followers, particularly the men and women in my Bible study group, started telling me that you—a scientist, a free-thinker, an atheist—were going to hell unless I saved you. I didn't leave the church because of their barbaric, dichotomous thinking so much as I couldn't yield to the discomforting irony: the man who unlocked the gates of hell and would fling you toward the opening was being "called" to intercept his own throw.

In regards to Greg Boyd, he once said that many of us view God as "Bad Santa." It makes sense. Santa provides the goods no matter how many times you pulled your sister's hair. He's the perfect vending machine: Your trivial good deeds are tokens that always assure a treat. God's tokens, which are in the form of prayers, are often ambiguous. Sometimes, the currency seems to have value; other times, none. But let's not claim Santa is better than God. Santa screwed me over, Elizabeth.

I think I just received a signal that it's time for me to get moving. I heard from behind me an RV's door open and a woman call, "Daddy and I are done watching porno movies. You can come back in now." The kids are cheering. Either they'd been waiting outside the RV all night, or their parents had banished them again sometime earlier. I hope it's the latter.

———————

I'm at another Denny's, this one in Taylorsville, Minnesota. I'm chewing Nicorette and waiting for my blueberry pancakes. I don't know what's taking them so long. There are only two other customers: a young man with an ID badge dangling from his neck and, across from him, a long-haired teenager wearing a Cannibal Corpse t-shirt. They're not saying anything to each other. My guess is the older guy is a social worker, and the kid is a delinquent. I can detect that kind of dynamic because when I was a teenager, I had a social worker too. Twice, he took me to the diner, and once we played basketball. I never saw him again after that. His assessment, I assume, was that I didn't need a mentor.

Minnesota is called the "Land of 10,000 Lakes." This description is a marketing ploy, a selling point for a state that—I suppose—isn't a national tourist's first choice. But they're not lying. There's one sweet lake after another; some as dark as an oil spill, others like sheets of tin foil. I can only admire beauty for so long, though. By the time I passed lake number twenty-three, I wanted to see desert. The truth is, no matter where I go, I'm disappointed. It's my parents' fault, for leaving me when I was four.

One night, Mom and Dad sat me and Molly down at the kitchen table. I imagined Dad was going to announce that the fire department had given him a raise and, as a result, we'd go to Disneyland. That's exactly what had happened when I was three, so why wouldn't it happen again? See, I was at the age when children start to recognize patterns, when they start believing that great things can happen more than once. Life hadn't yet revealed to me that only horrors repeat themselves.

Mom said, "Remember a few months ago at church when that mission came through?"

Yes. It was frigid and rainy. We sat under a blue tent in the parking lot. From the outside it appeared as exciting as a circus, but we found the activities on the inside were no more stimulating than watching mold grow. She continued, "That was a very important thing they were doing... coming into this country to preach. Because in China, they have to go to church in secrecy."

She explained, as best she could, how Catholicism had been more or less outlawed in China. I knew where the conversation was going: they'd ask me to make a card for some

Chinese boy. I'd write, *I'm sorry you can't have the Eucharist. I will pray for you.*

That's not what happened.

Something was clearly troubling Dad; he looked like he had a toothache. He cleared his throat and took a sip of his water. Then, after glancing at Mom, he said, "I'm retiring from the fire department in a month. After that, your mother and I are going to China."

Had I heard him correctly? Had he really said, "your mother and I" instead of "we"? I gasped. My chest tightened. Molly said, "No."

Mom said, "I feel like God is calling your father and me to do this."

Molly jumped in, "You mean we're not coming?"

My parents reasoned that it was too risky for children. Dad said, "We're not going long. Three months. That's it. Then we'll be back."

Molly said, "So, I'm babysitting? Does that mean I'll get paid?"

"No, no," chuckled Dad. "That would be a disaster. Grandpa and Aunt Eve will take care of you. You get along well with them. They'll move up here to the house. I know you're young and it's hard to understand, but in life there are things you just have to do, however odd they seem."

"But why you?" Molly said.

Dad answered, "Other people aren't brave enough. Believe me, this makes God happy, and he'll probably reward us, and reward you, too, for being so understanding. This is everyone's sacrifice."

Mom shook her head in agreement.

Molly said, "This doesn't make me happy."

My parents gazed at each other. Their eyes seemed sad, but I couldn't sympathize. I was feeling something new and profound, a stark realization that abandonment *can happen*, and it was happening to me. Dad said, "I hope that sooner or later it'll make sense. It will. These are the things that good adults do. Now listen…" He moved in closer. "I've had a lot of problems in my life. Fortunately, I took care of them long before you were born. But our sins stay with us until God offers us a chance to make penance. Helping people is a way for me to get right with God. I know that when I come back from this trip I'll be a new man, the father you've always wanted."

His rationalization meant nothing to me. The father I'd always wanted was the father I already had, not some pious idealist who'd discard his own son like a torn-off Band-Aid.

"Besides," said Mom. "You'll love being with Marvin and Eve."

Nothing they could say—no assurance or savvy feat of logic—could entice us to accept this crap. Mom and Dad were leaving. Everything I knew about my little world was going to change. God was misbehaving, taking instead of giving.

———

I'm at a truck stop in North Dakota, eating a Subway tuna sandwich. I've just gotten off the phone with Becky. The poor woman's been praying for me.

I said, "Hello, Becky, it's me, Wally. I called yesterday."

She giggled, "Did you think I'd forget you? I was praying all night for you. Are you still going north?"

"I'm still going north."

Over the truck stop's intercom, a voice said, "Showers number eight and nine are now open. If you have reserved showers number eight and nine, please go to showers number eight and nine."

I said, "Maybe I'm supposed to go north. Maybe I'm doing God's will. How do you know when you're doing God's will?"

She said, "When we're baptized, and we receive the Holy Spirit, our intuition is heightened. So usually, I can tell. Have you ever been baptized, Wally?"

I said, "When I was a baby. My parents were Catholics."

"I don't think there's a right or wrong way to worship, but as a Protestant, baptism is a choice. An act of free will."

"Right," I said. "Did I ever tell you why I'm going north?"

"You're running away from something."

"No. I'm running to something. Santa Claus."

"He's not real, Wally. Only Jesus is real. If you tell me where you are, I can try to find a local church that will—"

"You think I'm nuts," I said.

"No. I just think the devil's got you."

"My parents became missionaries in China. They left me with my abusive grandfather. It's hard to believe that God has a role in anything."

"It's a fallen world."

"I wish God would start over again, and do it right."

"He made everything right when he sent Jesus."

"Jesus didn't stop my grandfather."

"I'm sorry," she said. "I'll pray for you. I'll pray that Jesus shows you why that needed to happen, how it eventually would lead you to His love."

"I appreciate it. Can I call you again?"

"You can call any time."

"You'll always be there?"

"This is my home number, Wally. I'm doing this on my own."

"Why?"

She paused for a second. "It's a way for me to get right with God. By helping other people." My heart palpitated.

"Have you sinned?"

"I've sinned."

"Can you tell me what you've done?"

"I'm sorry, no. It's between me and God."

I said, "I understand. I'll pray for you."

When I hung up the phone, the voice on the intercom announced, "Showers number seven and six are now ready. If you have reserved showers number seven and six, please go to showers number six and seven."

I'm having a difficult time motivating myself to leave this truck stop. The two bored baristas at Coffee-On-The-Go keep glancing at me suspiciously. I've been sitting on a bench next to the tourist information kiosk for well over an hour. I'm having a moment of hesitation because in the next stretch of the journey, I'll be passing into Canada. Maybe I'm over-thinking this, but I feel like crossing the border metaphorically signifies the point of no return.

When I was planning this trip I focused more on the Santa angle. I didn't foresee how I'd end up dwelling on Marvin. He's been occupying my thoughts a lot, Elizabeth. Sometimes, I sense that he's more than just on my mind: he's in possession of it. I'm afraid to tell you the full story because, no offense, I don't think you have the experiential capacity to understand—or even visually conceptualize—my relationship with my grandfather. In the world of your childhood, grandfathers were synonymous with love.

Where I grew up, there was a significant asshole grandfather population. Go to the McDonald's on Route 59, and you'd find one heckling a lone teenage girl, commenting on her pubescence. Go to the Nanuet Mall, and you'd see a grandpa at the foot of the escalator, yelling to no one in particular, "I can't get on this stupid thing! Slow it down, you cocksuckers! I'm an old man for Christ's sake!" Go to a Chinese restaurant, and you'd see one sandwiched in a booth with his humiliated family, using his "outside" voice to explain to the waitress that although he'd shot a few gooks in Korea, he had the deepest sympathy because the war wasn't their fault: the Jews had orchestrated the whole thing. You'd find them trying to smoke cigarettes in the library; driving drunk at eight in the morning; in the church parking lot, whacking their wives' knees with their canes. They'd smack you in the head when you weren't looking; they'd throw their false teeth at you, then hand you their crusty snot rags to wipe the saliva off your shirt. They'd eat all the salami at family luncheons, get diarrhea, spray the furniture with shit, then beat grandma because it was her fault: she'd been a penny-pincher and bought the salami from that A-rab deli again, instead of the Italian.

I wish I could have met your grandfather. Even at my remove, his biography seemed captivating: a World War Two defector, an engineer at General Electric for thirty years, a Methodist minister for the last twenty years of his life. Although I've always been envious of how you admired him, your stories about his joviality, his warmth, his devotion to bringing happiness into the lives of others, instigated my deepest skepticism. How could I trust a happy story, given my background? I'd always thought you had a revisionist's memory. The trauma that he'd inflicted upon you must have been so profound that you created an Oprah-friendly fiction, a unique functional-family history, a genetic utopia of ideal filial forms. I respected you, though; I refused to shine a light upon your illusions because—other than a few harmless eccentricities—you showed no signs of neurosis.

Then, six months into our relationship, we drove to your parents' house in upstate New York to attend Thanksgiving with the Stolls. Here was a room full of people who leapt up and smiled whenever another relative arrived. You gathered each other into your arms, swept each other off the ground, rocked back and forth, and cried, "Oh, it's so good to see you!" By contrast, in my family, our bodies barely touched during hugs; we stood like A-frames.

Your family room bubbled with laughter. Nobody was drinking alcohol, yet somehow, everyone was cheerful. I waited for an outburst, for the as-yet-to-be-identified gene-pool degenerate to grab one of you by the neck and yell, "You shit fucker, I'll kill you!" It didn't happen. Whenever someone got up to pee, the conversations continued without gossip. When your 7-year-old nephew shattered a glass, Cousin Kurt didn't drag him outside and box the kid's ears until he was deaf. Instead, Kurt *helped* him clean up. He turned the disaster into an educational exercise, and they counted the shards of glass together. Either everyone was faking happiness, or my assumptions about your family were entirely wrong. It seemed unlikely—if not impossible—that so many people, spanning so many generations, could be complicit in such a complex performative conspiracy.

At dinner, Uncle Tyler offered a somber prayer in remembrance of Grandpa Stoll. Everyone bowed their heads.

Then, in flawless Methodist harmony, everyone sang "Amazing Grace." I swore an angel had stepped forward to conduct this chorus; the harmonies rolled and swirled, melodic patterns interlocking in a momentary dance, then releasing and tiptoeing away. The crescendo reached at the final chorus was so powerful that rifle shots would have seemed fitting. I moved my lips, but emitted no sound. I didn't know the words. Then, the song was finished. A silence came over the room. You turned to me and whispered, "We sang that at Pop-pop's funeral." (At Marvin's funeral, only the priest was allowed to sing. The song had nothing to do with Marvin; it was one of those Catholic liturgical standards about Christ raising the dead on the last day.)

Uncle Tyler forked turkey onto everyone's plates, and we passed around mashed potatoes. The steam tickled our cheeks. One of your cousins—the bearded geologist, I think—said, "Remember the time when Uncle Fray lost Pop-pop's hammer, and that Christmas Pop-pop got him like fifty different kinds of hammers?"

Mouths, everywhere, twitching, chortling. One of your cousins—the IT applications developer with the buttercup-yellow hair hanging over her shoulders—said, "Oh my God! I forgot about that. And he wrapped each and every one of them!"

Your father added, "In different kinds of paper!"

Aunt Betty said, "He was so thorough!"

Your family talked about Pop-pop like he was a mythological hero, the Odysseus of upstate New York, the Hermes of family gathering gags, the Prometheus of General Electric.

"Remember how he used to collect ice skates?" Uncle Tyler said. "Gosh, he'd drive us as far as Utica for a pair of old skates."

"He had hundreds of them," your father said, "stacked in the basement. What did we do with them after he died?"

Tyler said, "Didn't Betty take them?"

"I didn't take anything," Betty said. "Maybe Carl's got them?"

Carl, professor of Mathematics at Cazenovia College, looked up from his plate. "Huh? The skates? Mildred probably took them back to Buffalo. We'll have to ask her."

Finally, there was uncomfortable silence. I searched people's faces for signs of animosity, anything that would confirm that this Mildred person was a heartless bastard. I'd later find out that Mildred—whoever she was—had just received radioactive Iodine treatment. That's why she wasn't present. Here was further evidence that, in your family, conflict always came from without, and never from within.

Tyler, in an effort to recalibrate the initial bliss, said, "Remember when we were kids and the Mohawk River would freeze over and he'd ice skate to work?"

Smiles formed on everyone's lips. Tyler had succeeded in eliminating Mildred.

Your father added, "He'd skate all the way from Scotia!"

"They all thought he was nuts, but by February, every turbine engineer in the Capital District was skating down the Mohawk."

We pondered the image: scientists in lab coats gliding down the frozen river, their skates cutting onto the surface of the ice and leaving behind a trail of lines and dashes, their gloved hands clutching brief cases which swung with every stroke, their mouths debating over the most efficient way to achieve minimum kinetic friction, their arms extended at various angles in an effort to find the most advantageous posture for maintaining inertia. There was your grandfather, leading the exodus.

You said, "I remember when he used to read us his poetry before we'd all be put off to bed."

I thought, Christ, he was a poet, too?

Carl said, "Too bad he never tried to get any of it published. He was a darned good poet."

The geologist said, "Maybe we should, I don't know, make an anthology of his poetry? Or send some of his poems to literary magazines."

Your mother said, "My friend Ann from church choir has a daughter in school at Emerson. She reads for their literary journal. She's a screener or something. I can ask Ann about it."

Tyler said, "Remember that series of poems he wrote about Twinkle Toes?"

"Twinkle Toes! Twinkle Toes!" you said. "I used to go looking for him in the woods!"

The IT applications developer added, "I used to try to retell Pop-pop's Twinkle Toes stories to my friends on the playground, but I could never accurately mimic that, I don't know, alluring tone of his."

Your mother said, "He had a gift for storytelling!"

I reached for the water pitcher. I said, "So, who is Mildred, and what's her problem?"

Everything stopped. I could hear the wind outside. Your father pursed his lips, then Carl looked up from his plate, his blue eyes moving into mine. The geologist cleared his throat. Betty stared into her water glass. Your mother squinted sideways at the clock on the wall. Uncle Tyler rubbed his tongue against the inside of his cheek. You put your hand on my hip and smiled tentatively at everyone.

That day, I learned a lot about your grandfather, and your family learned a lot about me.

It looks like I'm staying in North Dakota tonight. When I arrived at this truck stop four hours ago, I'd intended on scribbling a short letter, no more than a page. Now, it's almost sundown. If I continue at this rate, a year will pass before I reach Inuvik. There's a Comfort Inn on the other side of the parking lot, but I'd rather not make a habit of running up the credit card, especially this early in the trip. I don't deserve comfort, anyway. I need to suffer for my poor time management skills.

There is one advantage to pulling an all-nighter at this truck stop: the environment has roused my ability to communicate with you honestly. My surroundings are sterile; this place was designed to be impersonal, cold, and so vast that no matter how crowded it becomes, it'll always feel empty. Nothing here is inviting but for the exit signs. Yet my pen moves in urgent rebellion against the imposed banality, as if my memories and confessions might fill this vacuous space. My inspiration is compensation. Such fluidity could never occur in a cozy motel.

Now, back to grandfathers. Your family terrified me. I couldn't imagine spending the next fifty or sixty Thanksgivings and Christmases around people who insisted on being happy.

I thought that once we'd moved to Cincinnati for your graduate studies, I'd be safe from the folklore of perfect grandfathers. But, two months after we'd moved into our tiny apartment, your father paid us a surprise visit. He'd driven all the way from New York to deliver a piano. It was a wedding gift from your grandfather. Eight years prior, within a few days of his death, he'd told your father to give the piano to you once you got married.

We stood at the curbside, by the U-Hall's open back. Our neighbors gazed out their windows, squinted their eyes so they could see what was in the U-Hall's dark interior. Your father's cheeks took on that particular red hue that only appeared during moments of unbelievable generosity. Incidentally, his cheeks were almost always that color.

You people, you Stolls, gave and gave and gave and expected nothing in return. You Methodists, you exemplars of unconditional love and amazing grace, with your God who blesses both the righteous and the rotten. In your family, belief meant *being*. Spirituality was a behavior, not a guilt-complex or sustained fear of God reaching down and flicking you. Would my parents have gone to China had they been Methodists? Was it guilt, not grace, that pulled them out of my life? Would I not be running away from you right now and chasing down Santa Claus had I lived in the spirit of a Wesleyan community, rather than being reverent to a far-away Pope, and alienated from God's love through my wickedness?

I recall the hot tears rolling down your face that day, how you flung yourself against your father, arms encircling him. He said, "Pop-pop wanted me to keep it a secret, to wait until you got married."

The piano was amazing, but I wondered where the hell we'd put the thing. Even though it was an upright, we simply didn't have room for it in our apartment.

After that weekend, what had once been our office—the sacred cave where I composed my largely misunderstood plays—became the music room. Searching for another genius-accommodating sanctuary, I dragged my desk to the closet. It didn't fit. I hauled the desk out to the curb, and stuck a For Sale sign on it. That night, someone came by and just took it. They left the For Sale sign on the lawn.

For months you encouraged me to play the piano, but I kept telling you that I wasn't interested. The truth, Elizabeth, is that I couldn't bring myself to touch the keys. Let me explain.

Some nights, while you were sleeping, I'd wander past the music room on my way to the kitchen. I'd stop at the door and gaze at the piano, only able to discern its shape in the darkness. I'd imagine Pop-pop sitting on the piano bench, all the Stolls gathered around him in a semicircle. I'd see a fireplace crackling in the background and blue moonlight glowing on the frosty window. A dog sleeping on a bundled up quilt. Family photo albums spread out along the floor, momentarily abandoned for the spontaneous joy of music. I could hear your family singing old church hymns, arms around each other, bodies swaying together:

> *Come, and let us sweetly join*
> *Christ to praise in hymns divine;*
> *give we all with one accord*
> *glory to our common Lord.*

I could not allow my evil hands to touch and defile that sacred object. Not only would I imbue the piano with my depraved energy, but, considering the consequences of a similar act of irreverence, found in 2 Samuel 2:6, it would be in my best interest to keep my hands in my pockets:

Uzzah reached out and took hold of the ark of God, because the oxen stumbled. The Lord's anger burned against Uzzah because of his irreverent act; therefore God struck him down and he died there beside the ark of God.

Heck, God even killed seventy men of Beth Shemesh because they had *looked at* the ark!

I kept to my commitment. Not once was I tempted to tap a key. After a few months, the piano's presence was no more consuming than the mothballs in our linen closet.

But then, things changed. Kyle knocked on our door one Wednesday night. He had come for a piano lesson. I had forgotten about your arrangement. I'd thought that it was just one of those tentative plans that friends make, the kind that never reaches fruition, that lingers perpetually in the indeterminate "we should."

When Kyle arrived, I was on the couch eating Cheez-Its. Orange crumbs and salt grains dotted my shirt and lap. I was watching the History Channel, a documentary on Nebuchadnezzar II's invasion of Jerusalem in 578 BCE and the destruction of Solomon's Temple.

"Who's that?" I called.

"Remember?" you said. "Kyle's taking piano lessons."

No, I thought. This cannot be happening. Bewildered, I glanced back at the television. White men, dressed as Babylonians, were dragging the King of Judah out of an underground chamber in Solomon's Temple. In the background was a purple curtain, which presumably concealed the Ark of the Covenant. One of the Babylonian thugs, eager to desecrate, clutched the golden menorah from the center of the room and tossed it at the curtain.

I wondered: after an army defeated its foes and set about routine pillaging, did the warriors fight among themselves to be the first to defile the enemy's temples? Did friends and cohorts spear each other in the guts as they plundered sacred stockpiles? Was there a kind of honor—one that stayed in the family for generations—to attain by debasing the rival's hallowed treasures?

I thought of Kyle's fingers. Those fucking evil digits. Those germy little Babylonian beasts leading a conquest to lay the Stoll family artifacts to waste. Those vulgar fingers, the emails he'd typed:

> *Wally, in the thirty-one years that you've been alive, someone must have showed you how to use Excel. Am I correct? It's really not that hard. Matter of fact, it's designed to accommodate even the most pedestrian mind. That said, the Post-Event Financial Statement you delivered to the Treasury and Trust Board was, by all means, aesthetically offensive. Difficult to read, cluttered, improperly balanced. Who uses bold, underline, and italics all at once? You. Who still uses Impact font? You. This is the kind of work that a mildly retarded entry-level data-entry "technician" would compose three minutes before his lunch break. We're not idiots, Wally. We're professionals.*

Those pompous, boorish fingers would touch our piano keys, the ark that contained your grandfather's soul.

I threw my Cheez-Its aside and tried to rush to the music room so that I could christen the piano with my lesser sin, but Kyle stopped me, handed me his jacket, and said, "I don't know where your coat closet is."

"It's in my office," I said, wanting to hand it back, but hesitant because you were watching.

He preempted my every attempt to get to the piano, as if he knew my motives. "How about a glass of wine?" he said. "What kind of host are you? Oh, don't look so sour! I'm just pulling your leg. Always so serious, Wally!"

I fished out the manager's-special wine that we kept beneath the sink, that pulpy and sulfuric sludge I'd forgotten to throw out two years before, after a half-glass had scorched your throat and left you farting for three days.

After I handed Kyle his glass, you tugged my arm and said, "Can you do me a favor? I picked up some sheet music today, and left it in the car. You mind grabbing it?"

Either you had an incredibly coincidental and inconvenient sense of timing, or you were complicit in the plot to prohibit me from touching the piano. I don't know what kind of face I made, but you said, "I cooked dinner tonight, and it was your day off. The least you could do—"

"OK! OK!" I said.

Kyle, amused at our bickering, sipped his wine, then licked his lips. "Not bad. Not bad at all," he said. "Let me guess. Southern France? Maybe Bordeaux?"

When I came back with the sheet music, he was already tapping the piano keys. You were sitting next to him on the bench, your hips touching. Two temples destroyed in a matter of seconds. The sheet music fell from my hands.

———————

Here's something to consider: after your father delivered the piano, you played it every day for a few months, but then stopped. "I have no time," you claimed. It was all graduate school. Back then, you were just embarking on the path that would lead to your theory of the B-Gravitrope. You felt the presence of some great unknown—could it be a more efficient way to simulate baryon asymmetry? An explanation for fermion mass regularities? Sometimes, you spent twelve hours at the lab, would come home, microwave a vegetarian burrito, nap for thirty minutes, then rush back to campus. On weekends, our apartment became a maze of dry erase boards. Everywhere I looked, Greek symbols, numbers, arrows, lines, brackets, and parentheses. One board—with its unfinished equation—would be connected to another via thread. The strings crisscrossed our living room, ran through the kitchen, looped along the music room. The Minotaur in this maze had died and the spiders safely spun their cobwebs.

The piano remained untouched.

What, then, after several years, reanimated the music that had been dormant in your soul? What reunited you with your family's spirit?

Kyle.

After Kyle's first lesson, you created a new habit. You practiced alone every evening, between dinner and study time. You acquired new beliefs: baroque music had the power to increase concentration. I'd find you at the piano, so focused, so intent, so diligent. I was unable to escape the Kyle-envy that dominated my thoughts. I'd sit next to you and start pounding on the keys like I was punching my grandfather. The first time, you gave a sideways smile, like it was a cute little joke. The fifth time, you pushed me and told me to leave you alone. You said, "No, Wally."

I'd wished that you would have said, "Instead of treating the piano the way a child does, why don't you sit down and I'll teach you a song?"

Then came that night. Thirty minutes after Kyle left, and you were still playing away. I was in the other room, watching *Spiderman II* and entertaining vulgar fantasies of Kirsten Dunst. Whatever you were playing was so beautiful that I shut the TV off and listened. You touched each note gently, like you were plucking diamonds from heaven. As the soft melody rippled, I felt tears welling in my eyes. I wanted to leap up and embrace you, tell you that you'd struck the chord on the magic harp, that nothing will ever stand between my love for you again.

I stood in the doorway to the music room. "What are you playing?" I said. My voice fluttered.

You looked straight ahead, fingers still moving. "'Trees' by Kieko Matsui," you said. "Isn't it lovely?"

I stepped inside the room and sat beside you. I was going to say, "Teach me this song," but I noticed something horrible. I smelled Kyle all over you.

And what was I to do but embrace my family history, like you had embraced yours. I don't know what came over me, Elizabeth. Nobody in my family ever knows what comes over us. When I reached for the key guard and slammed it down on your hands, it wasn't me. Your reflexes weren't quick enough: your fingers leapt back no more than a few millimeters, but that arbitrary distance, coupled with the descending key guard's kinetic strength, had forced your fingers to land on discordant notes. To me, those jarring intervals and the rhythmic cacophony of knuckles shattering sounded familiar and therefore pleasant. Familiar to what? I couldn't tell because it wasn't me. I swear to God that it wasn't me. It was Marvin. Only he would seek to hear those hellish sounds.

You screeched, rushed out of the room so fast that your eyeglasses fell off. I heard the bathroom door lock, the water running, and your sobs. Despite the sound of your crying—so familiar to my childhood—I failed to comprehend the reality of what I'd just done. I stayed seated at the piano, lifted the key guard. I stared at the keys, a few of them speckled with blood. I reached down and played a C chord.

July 29

Getting into Canada took two hours. The border cops seized my passport and pulled me over to an area designated for suspicious people. They searched the car and found an empty pill bottle that had been under the seat for a year. They asked what my medicine was for. I said, "I'm unipolar."

The customs woman said, "What's unipolar?"

I said, "I don't know. It's what my doctor told me I have. Back in 1999, when I was living in Syracuse, New York, when I couldn't even keep jobs in retail, the memory foam in my head began to bubble. Three different psychiatrists told me that I'm bipolar. Based on the latest diagnosis—"

The woman handed me the bottle and said, "Just get going."

I'm at St. Malo Provincial Park now. The lake is a saliva-filled horse pond compared to Devil's Lake. Across the campsite are a group of college kids. They're blasting Phish and having a party. I'd like to join them, but I'd end up smoking all their pot. The odor is alluring, some kind of sweet and expensive variety. You know you've got good weed when the smoke refuses to dissipate. It interacts with the air like a slab of meat. I miss getting high. Marijuana is one of the few things in the world that I know how to do without fucking it up.

Instead of doing drugs, I'm reading *Shakespeare's Plays: A Collection with Essays*. Kyle loaned me this book when he realized that I knew almost nothing about Shakespeare. Although I was a theater major in college, we'd only done one Shakespeare production during my time there. The department chair, Dr. Otis, was one of those weirdoes who believed that Shakespeare wasn't Shakespeare; rather, he thought the playwright was a secret committee of anti-Protestant conspirators. Dr. Otis favored Shakespeare's contemporaries instead. Inferior fellows like Marlowe and Johnson and Middleton and Fletcher. I speak as if I know this stuff. Keep in mind that my graduating GPA was 2.3.

Remember how stupid I was when we met? I barely ever read. All I did was huff chronic, eat Cheetos, and watch TV.

———————

Have you noticed that in Shakespeare's plays everyone starts off fucked up? They go out into the woods, experience calculated pandemonium, and then return feeling much better. Is that not the perfect formula for a well-lived life? Although I've torn our memory foam in two, taken the money and the better car, I want to come back out of the woods with no complaints.

Consider this, too: Shakespeare believed that love is only ideal when it's on a stage. That's one reason why I'm taking this trip. Certainly, I have not been the model husband, the exemplar of conjugal love, so, in order to embody your ideal—our ideal, really—I've taken it upon myself to perform the virtues of love, to enact the matrimonial responsibilities that would have otherwise eluded me had I remained home. By getting in the car, driving far away, and protecting you from my turbulent introspection; by sending you honest letters; by stepping onto the stage and facing you, my sole audience, my soul mate, I'm becoming the all-loving, all-honest character I was meant to be. The theory goes that if you play the role well enough, the role will eventually play you. And soon, when I pull into our parking spot and get out of the car, weary from the journey but renewed forever, you'll immediately discover the flaw in Shakespeare's aphorism: when ideal love is achieved on stage, the proscenium vanishes, the divide between audience and player becomes indistinguishable, every wall becomes the fourth wall, and all the world does, indeed, become a stage. The only things remaining are the characters, and this character—Wally Tiparoy—casted as the ideal husband, will run to you with his arms open.

You're thinking, "Nonsense. You can't embody something that isn't there inherently. At most, you'll be imitating. You'll tire of it, sooner or later. Plus, if you have to perform love, then that love is insincere."

While I agree—shamefully—that loving virtues might not be inherent to my nature, both you and I know nature's composition can be altered by intention alone. Remember the neutron? It didn't exist until James Chadwick dreamed it up and looked for it. Then, suddenly, it always existed. If it can happen in science, it can happen in a marriage. I simply don't believe reality is fixed. It changes, it misbehaves, it farts and burps, just like we do. It goes out into its woods of people and returns with contentment.

———

Hours have passed. I'm writing by the Coleman lantern. The gas is hissing, and moths are circling the light. They keep bumping into my forehead. The Phish fans kept me up for several hours, but they've finally passed out. I'd considered walking over to their camp and asking them to turn their stereo down, but I didn't want to seem like an old poop. Then again, I could have recovered my credibility by noting that they were listening to a live performance from July 12, 2000, at Deer Creek Music Center in Indiana. It was a memorable and humorous show because, in the second set, Phish played Led Zeppelin's "Moby Dick" after every song, a total of six times. In my imagination, these kids would have revered me as a God—a walking, talking Phish archive. But let's be real. They probably would have thought, "This old loser is trying to be hip." Even if they were impressed by my knowledge, they'd eventually ask, "So what do you do now?"

That would have killed it. I'd have crushed their liberal idealism by proving that middle-class culture has the power to appropriate Phish Heads. I'd seem downright pathetic when I'd confess that I haven't listened to Phish since getting married, that I'd thrown the bong out because pot smoking interfered with my productivity. Or I'd become so overcome by nostalgia that I'd ask for a few bowl hits, then start yapping unremittingly about pointless matters, like how CVS's interior layout appeals to Marxists, or how it's impossible to envision a hole without a rim. So I suffered. I listened to "Moby Dick" six times.

Now, of course, I'm writing you. I want to talk about Grandpa Marvin, but something keeps distracting me. There's a row of hedges about sixty feet away, separating my campsite from the gravel road. I swear the hedges are rotating in unison, but only when I'm not looking at them. I hear a rustle, I glance up, and their positions seem to have changed, like they've spun on their axes. Some look a little wider at the base, with maybe a few extra branches jutting out, and their poorly rounded tops take on an altogether dissimilar shape with each twist.

I'm tired; I'm probably hallucinating, but still, it worries me. Like when I saw that baby in the Denny's parking lot nodding his head at me.

July 30

My back feels like twisted plywood. I wasn't inspired to write much today; I'm too depressed. I spent ten hours driving through Saskatchewan, thinking that if you were here with me, you'd uplift my spirits. You'd point out all the things that I failed to notice, like the wind-slanted birch trees and stark-red lilies on Highway 16. You'd note how the fathomless sky reflects the plains and sand dunes to the west and looks like tarnished brass. You'd love it because in Cincinnati we always felt restricted, like there's a Hefty bag pulled across the atmosphere, holding in all the soot and smog and unspoken words.

The crazy thing is that even without you here, I've started to notice all the things that I wouldn't have noticed unless you were here. That's a bit clunky. Let me clarify: I was experiencing the world as if you were by my side. It was a feeling that I rarely encountered in our lives together, even when we were literally side-by-side. Does that mean I'm changing? Am I finally procuring the kind of empathy that enables normal married people to express love and adoration toward each other? Keeping with the metaphor, is my perception of the world's oppressive enormity collapsing in direct proportion to my sudden yearning for you? That's what I want, Elizabeth. It's exactly what I want!

It's 11:30PM and I'm at Pike Lake Park. The wind is moving in circular gusts, like a procession of boulders rolling down a hill. On my way to the campsite, I bought a tent at Wal-Mart because last night was hell. There were too many flies circling my head, and spiders crawling up the backs of my legs. Several times, a raccoon wandered over to me. I had to jump up to shoo it away, and then it would come back again, just as I was falling asleep.

It took me thirty minutes to put the tent up, and now it's billowing in the gust, each gale a fist bashing the canvas. I can't keep my mind aligned tonight; it's revolting against the never-ending straight road my body followed all day. I have to try to sleep. I'm sorry that I have nothing else to say. I'm just feeling so miserably tired.

July 31

So, this morning, I took the tent I bought and threw it out on the roadside. I'm done with camping. Tonight, I'm staying at Dave's Inn in Grande Prairie, Alberta. Yes, I put it on the card, but don't worry: a single meal at Panera Bread costs more than a room here. To give you an idea of just how sordid this place is, about an hour after I checked in, the alarm clock on the nightstand started flashing. I couldn't get it to stop, so I went to unplug it. I had to squat, reach under the bed, and pull the electrical cord from the outlet. I noticed a discarded shoe under the bed. For the next ten minutes, I inspected the rest of the room. I found a chicken bone under the seat cushion, a bag full of melted crayons on the closet's top shelf, and dead spiders in every crevice and corner. Were circumstances different, I would have left. I'm too tired to care. Notwithstanding last night's insomnia, today was horribly long.

I woke up depressed and irritable, and carried it with me all morning. At about noon, I called Becky again. I thought that maybe she could uplift my spirits. Maybe we could get real, and she'd finally tell me what big sin had prompted her to become a Christian.

This time, the payphone was outside, at a gas station, and I couldn't talk for long with the never-ending windstorm thrashing me about. She said, "Wally, where are you?"

"Somewhere in Alberta, Canada. I don't know and I don't really care."

An updraft nearly rolled me over. It swung back and hit me from the other direction. She said, "You sound distressed."

"I am. Hey, have you thought about telling me what your big sin was?"

"No, Wally, I haven't, and I won't."

"It would be easier for me to find Jesus if I could relate to someone else's wickedness."

She said something that sounded like, "We're all wicked," but I couldn't be sure. The wind was too loud, so forceful that a metal garbage can rolled by like a bowling ball.

I said, "I can't hear you."

"I can't hear you either."

"I'll call you tonight. Can you please pray to Jesus and ask him if you should tell me about your sins?"

I heard no response. I said, "They're just sins. What's the big deal? Paul told us that we need to be open with each other."

Dial tone. Either she was annoyed and hung up, or she thought I'd said goodbye.

I returned to the car, got back on the highway, and began what felt like the longest stretch of the trip so far. Spread out before me was an endless checkerboard of rippling wheat and prairie grass. Occasionally, cornfields would rupture the monotony with their dilapidated farmhouses, grain silos, and rusty tractors, but they were sparse. When my eyes grew tired, I focused on the warship-shaped clouds that loomed on the horizon. I couldn't catch up to them; they were receding quicker than I was driving. My car swayed in the gusts, and the air rushing through the open window tasted like cayenne pepper. Through the heavy static on the radio, I heard brief, distant bursts of Elvis. I jogged the tuner, hoping to hone in on a strong signal. Who was I to think that clarity would be attainable out here? The laws of nature insisted that this stretch of land remain mundane, that nothing of distinction or substance emerge from the static. I felt like I was on my own. Yesterday's optimistic sense that we were spiritually side-by-side was long gone. I detected a psychic disturbance in our universe. Maybe you'd given up on me. Maybe Kyle had egged you on and said, "You've got to leave that unstable freak, Liz. He's going to ruin your life."

About two hours into the second leg of my day's journey, I saw a blank billboard in the prairie. I recalled the empty picture frame in Kyle's office. I'd been thinking about him a lot over the last few hours.

I'm sorry that I was suspicious. It's just that, well, you always laugh when you're around him, and it makes me crazy. You've known him for seven years and you haven't gotten tired of his jokes. But with me, after six months of marriage, you couldn't even produce a contrived chuckle. If there's one thing that I've learned from all my past relationships, it's that I should start packing my bags when my lover no longer finds my jokes funny.

Let's be honest. I want to know why you've remained friends with Kyle. Sure, it made sense seven years ago, when you went through that little Unitarian phase and he "mentored" you, but after you've seen how he's treated me at work—the forced overtime, his passive aggressive sense of intellectual and cultural superiority, and his refusal to consider my "uninformed" ideas—I don't get why you and Kyle have remained friends. Because he's smart? Because he has an appreciation for obscure French shit? Because he understands physics? Because—by implication of his love for Shakespeare—he's romantic and expressive?

Listen: your knight in shining armor wishes that he can encase your body in plaster, all but for a small hole where your legs meet. He doesn't want you to move. He doesn't want you to speak. He just wants to snort coke and penetrate you. Despite all the enlightening midnight phone conversations you've had with Kyle about sociology and science, he's had one outcome in mind: your fuckable immobilization. Don't trust him.

I'm lying in bed, but I still feel like I'm moving at 60MPH. When I close my eyes, I see advancing asphalt. If I ever become rich—if some open-minded New York theatrical producer options one of my plays and makes it a Tony Award winner— I'm going to write out a check to Dave's Inn. I'm going to scribble on the memo line, "Buy new mattresses. The ones you have now are banana-shaped and they smell like armpits."

There's a truck idling outside my window. The thermal curtains stifle the engine's roar, making it sound like monks chanting on the other side of the glass.

The truck has been there an hour. The driver is talking on his CB radio. His signal is so strong that my room's television antenna is picking up his conversation. The TV only receives one channel, which is airing a documentary on 2012 doomsday predictions. I see volcanoes erupting, computer generated images of Manhattan cracking in half, and I hear the trucker attempting to arrange an anonymous encounter with a hooker.

"I'm not baiting you, honey," he says. "I'm not like that."

On the television, Nostradamus scribbles on parchment.

Now I'm thinking about the end of the world, from the Christian perspective, and that I should call back Becky.

––––––––––––––

Seven years ago, when you started attending the Unitarian church and I retaliated, briefly, by going to a Christian mega-church, you became worried. You didn't want me to get brainwashed, to start preaching salvation, to denounce science and sex and liberalism. You were afraid that I lacked the mental fortitude to investigate Christianity objectively. Sweethearts like Becky remind me exactly why I ultimately rejected Christianity.

I called her again. "Hey," I said. "Did you hang up on me this afternoon?"

"I thought you hung up on me."

"It must have been the wind," I said.

"Or God's disapproval of our conversation."

The trucker's voice came out of the TV. "I don't have a lot of money," he said, "so it all depends on what you can do for a couple of dollars."

Becky continued, "But I thought about it and prayed. This morning when I turned the radio to my favorite Christian rock station, I heard a song on about being open and honest. So I guess God's giving me the nudge, telling me that I should tell you what brought me to Jesus."

The trucker said, "Then I don't want your business, you dirty skank."

I said, "Right, but if you don't feel comfortable—"

"When I was a teenager, working at Macy's, this woman… well, she shopped there a lot and always went out of her way to talk to me. One day we went out for coffee. I ended up back in her apartment, and, um, we took our clothes off and kissed and rubbed."

"So you're a lesbian?" I asked. I wondered if she could hear me smiling.

"No, Lord no! It was a one-time thing, but an abomination nonetheless. Satan was working through her."

"Becky," I said. "That's not a sin!"

"It's a sin. Let me get my Bible—"

"Don't even," I laughed. "No matter what Paul has to say, it's not a sin! The Bible was written a long time ago, and Paul was responding to—what?—the Greeks tying up little boys and keeping them as sex slaves? It's all about historical context."

"I read the living Bible. The word of God is eternal, Wally."

"Heck, maybe if you look at your affair more objectively, you might find that you actually liked the experience."

I heard a thud. She might have dropped her Bible. "Like? Like? How could someone actually *like* same sex—"

"You need to lighten up on yourself. It's not a huge deal."

"It's a sin!" she hollered. "I've sinned, Wally. I've offended the Lord! This is *my* sin, my act of desecration, my pact with the devil. Don't you dare tell me otherwise!"

"OK. Sorry. I'm not trying to play devil's advocate or anything. Just giving you the humanist's perspective."

She said, "I'm not letting go of this one. The last thing I want to do is to start rationalizing it. That's taking the path right back to Satan. What I did was wrong, but it led me to Jesus, and if it wasn't for Jesus taking care of the eternal consequences of my sin, I'd be riding the grease pole to hell. You understand? It was a sin."

I paused. As nuts as Becky sounded, I felt like I could

relate to her. For the two of us, expressing and embracing love is damnation.

The truck driver's voice came out of the TV again: "Breaker one-nine, this is Snakeskin. Any of you boys got ten dollars I can borrow?"

I said, "I understand. Yes, yes, it was a sin."

"Good. Now let's put that behind us and talk about your relationship with Jesus."

"Next time," I said.

"What do you mean next time? I just told you my darkest secret. The least you can do is discuss Jesus for a few minutes."

"Right, but I feel like the Lord is calling me to do something immediately. There's someone nearby who's in need."

She didn't respond.

I said, "Becky, I have to go."

"Go, then. If you feel like God is telling you to do something, then go do it." The excitement in her voice was gone. She must have thought I was the most challenging caller she'd ever had. Or maybe I was her only caller.

I said goodbye, hung up, and rummaged through my backpack for my wallet. I plucked out a ten-dollar bill and headed outside, where the horny trucker was waiting for some charity.

Now, as I lie on this stinky, concave mattress, in a bed that was made for two, I hear the truck motor's unending croon and think, "At least someone is getting laid tonight."

———

You know what I liked? I liked that time when you and I had sex outside in the rain. You were on summer break from school, and I was unemployed. We'd pitched a tent up in the Adirondacks. It poured for three days, and finally we said fuck it, let's fuck outside. Let's be at one with nature in every possible way. Our backs were muddy, our knees were scraped up, our bodies black and blue from all the roots we rolled over, but it was beautiful.

August 1

I drove for about six hours today. I didn't get far because I blew a tire. Something strange happened while I was getting the tire changed at Wal-Mart, but I'll tell you about that later, after I've processed it. Right now, I'm in Fort Nelson, near British Columbia's western tip. I'm staying at the Moonlight Inn, another cheap dump. I thought everything north of Calgary would be covered in glaciers, but the weather is still mild. This city looks no different from Cincinnati.

Several years ago, a band from Fort Nelson had a hit song. They were called Movie Flow. I wanted their CD but couldn't afford it because I was only making eight dollars an hour. That's how much Kyle thought I was worth. You were researching antisymmetric matter, making $9,000 a year with a graduate fellowship. That year, we learned a lot about not getting the things that we desired.

I was used to that, of course. Even before I'd been denied Soundwave, I had suspicions that life might become horribly disappointing. Three months after my parents had left for China, Marvin started to act antsy. Up until then, he was indifferent about his babysitting role. Most days, he watched cable TV. Occasionally, he took Molly and me to the mall or up to Rockland Lake. He was quiet, only talked when necessary, and rarely complained about the messes we'd made or how we tended to be hyperactive and loud in the evening.

But once that three-month mark had come, that moment when my parents had asked him—directly or indirectly—to extend the terms of his contact, he started to pace about the house, grumbling to himself. Some days, he'd just stare out the window.

One afternoon, when I'd just gotten home from school, I sat at the kitchen table for my snack. We'd been learning about family in Mrs. Muller's class, and I was eager to ask Marvin some questions. He was at the counter, back turned, hands busy preparing my peanut butter and jelly sandwich. I said, "Is my great-great grandfather your father?"

"Yup," he said.

"What was he like?"

"He worked on a barge. He had a peg-leg, like a pirate."

I said, "Did he get hurt? Bit by a shark?"

His voice deepened. "No. It was an accident."

"Was he mad at you?"

"For what?"

"The accident."

Marvin lifted his head. He stared at the open cupboard in front of him, hands motionless. Then, "I didn't say that I caused the accident." He spun around and glared at me. "Is that what you heard?" The lines in his face had become deeper and darker, his wrinkles now gashes.

"No."

"Then why did you ask that?"

"I dunno?"

His jaw moved back and forth a few times, eyes still locked onto me. "You know, your father used to ask me a lot of questions. All the time, one question after another. He wouldn't stop. So I made him stop."

He turned back to my sandwich and said, "Do they tell you in school that there's no such thing as a stupid question?"

"Yeah."

"They're wrong. You just asked me a stupid question. How am I supposed to deal with that? What do you think I should do?" He cracked his knuckles.

"Forgive me?"

I must have hit a nerve. He slammed his fist onto the counter. The glasses and mugs inside the cupboard rattled, and immediately, from the living room, Aunt Eve called, "What was that?"

"Nothing," he hollered. "Mind your own business."

He slowly looked over his shoulder at me. "Forgiveness. Guess your father drilled that one into your head, right? Mad at me all his life because I told him the truth one day. See, we allow stupid questions—we don't want to hurt your precious feelings by pointing out that what you say is plain dumb—but we won't tolerate being frank and honest. Me, I never believed in that. In my family, we say it like it is."

He looked back at my sandwich. He popped the lid off the grape jelly.

"So," he said, "One day, your father was rattling off all these questions. Stupid things like 'What did Abe Lincoln eat that made him so big?' I say, 'How the hell am I supposed to answer that?' He says, 'You're my dad. You're supposed to know.' Whoever told him that fathers know everything should be shot. I say, 'Look, Anthony. I might be your father, but I didn't want to have you. Neither did your grandmother. You were an accident. Keep that in mind whenever you talk to me.'"

It didn't make sense. How could a child be an accident? How could a father not want his son?

I heard the butter knife skid over the bread. He scooped more jelly out of the jar, the knife clanking on the glass rim. Marvin continued, "It runs in the family, I guess. You know your father and mother didn't want to have you? You were an accident, too."

I felt like the room was tipping sideways. My ears rang. This was my first experience of cognitive dissonance, and it would have gotten worse had Aunt Eve, unbeknownst to Marvin and me, not been standing at the kitchen's entrance.

"Marvin," she said, so monotone, so devoid of emotion.

He watched her. She picked up the phone that was mounted to the kitchen wall. He put the knife down gently and wiped his hands on a towel. Her index finger was in the rotary wheel, the phone's coiled cord swinging at her side. He walked to her, grabbed her index finger, and bent it backwards. With his other hand, he pulled the cradle away from her ear, then yanked on it so hard that the cord ripped out of the phone jack.

She didn't wail. She didn't resist.

He whispered, "Don't you have some gardening to do?"

He let go of her index finger. She walked away.

I don't remember what I was thinking, Elizabeth. I wasn't equipped with the kind of vocabulary that could make sense of what had transpired. Because it would later occupy my thoughts so much, I was probably wondering if I'd really been an accident.

I looked at Marvin. His back was turned again. He reached for the bottle of Ajax by the sink. He held it over my open sandwich and shook.

I watched the blue cloud descend from the bottle and land on the peanut butter.

You're shocked. You're wondering why I never told you this. It's because you're practical, scientific. You know too much about heredity and biological determinism. You'd be scared that you married another Marvin.

"That's Ajax," I said. "You can't eat Ajax."

He said, "Again, you're making assumptions. Saying something stupid. Maybe I happen to store sugar in an old Ajax bottle?"

"It's—"

"Sugar. It's sugar, Wally." He folded the bread together and brought me the plate.

I stared at the sandwich.

"For Christ's sake, eat it! It's fucking sugar, Wally. What the hell is wrong with you?"

I wanted to open the sandwich and show him the blue granules, but I was scared. He might bend my finger back like he did Eve's. He might tell me more things that I didn't want to know. I bit into the sandwich. I chewed. Moments later, my gums began to sting and my tongue went numb. Marvin, satisfied, walked upstairs and closed the bedroom door. I sat at the table and cried.

That was the first time I ever thought about revenge. Specifically, I imagined entering the bathroom when Marvin was in the shower, and swiping his feet out from under him.

———

I don't feel like talking about Marvin anymore tonight. There's only so much painful recollection I can take. Besides, I need to tell you about what happened when I went to get the tire replaced.

I had the blowout on the Alaska Highway, just north of the Muskwa River Bridge. On a doughnut, I made it to a Wal-Mart in Fort Nelson. As I waited for the mechanics, the attendant said, "I haven't seen a tourist come through here in a while."

I told him that I wasn't a tourist, but a photojournalist for a foreign relations magazine. What I should have said was, "I'm a meat-based computer. I serve no practical function other than to take up space and wreak havoc in the lives of those who love me." I should have told him that when I unwrap myself, my chest becomes a cassette player, just like Soundwave's. I should have told him that my wife is a human slab of meat named Elizabeth. I'd say, "She's about to travel the country giving lectures on dark matter rotational curves. She discovered the B-Gravitrope." I'd tell him it's been ages since I've been stoned, and then I'd ask him where I could score some El Niño. I'd mention that according to a book sold at Barnes & Noble, the universe aligns itself with our intentions when we meditate on what we want. What I really said was, "I'm documenting a political rally at the North Pole."

"North Pole?" he said. He pointed toward the northeast side of the automotive section, where the floormats hung on silver arms like disconnected tongues. "The North Pole is that way. Way, way, that way. You're a bit off."

"I know. But in my version of reality, everything is hundreds of miles away from where it should be."

His eyebrows arched. He looked away and cleared his throat.

I sat in the automotive station's waiting room and watched the greasy men stick their hands into the guts of a battered SUV. I picked up an issue of *Hollywood Life*. The main article was on the actress Kirsten Dunst's hard-core party habits. One photograph showed her exiting a New York rock club, cigarette hanging from her lips, her face pale. She was drunk. Last year, her eyes looked like polished emeralds, and now they were slush and mud. Poor girl.

Then her lips moved.

"Shit," I said to myself. "I need some sleep."

They moved again. She said something, but I didn't hear it. I looked closer. They parted and quivered, and when I held my ear to the picture, I heard, "Your wife can stomach a lot, but you've gone too far, Wally."

I slammed the magazine shut and whispered to my brain. "I'm not going to let you do this to me. I'm a normal human being who can function in the world just fine without medical help. I won't let you sabotage this journey."

My legs began to shake. Lack of sleep, I told myself.

Another customer entered. I made believe that nothing had happened. He sat next to me and, in a complete breach of social etiquette, extended his hand for a shake. "Hello," he said. I wondered if that was typical Canadian behavior. I didn't want to be an ass, so I reciprocated.

His name was Elroy. He was an old man with, apparently, a keen ability to discern accents. He said, "You sound like you're from Columbus, Ohio? Or is it Cincinnati?"

I threw the magazine on top of the stack. Talk to him, I told myself, still bewildered by Kirsten's comment. "Good guess. I live in Cincinnati, but originally I'm from New York. I moved out there when my wife got into graduate school," I said.

"It's a nice place. I used to drive there for business, but I'm retired now."

As I asked Elroy what kind of work he did, I shuffled the magazines and hid *Hollywood Life* somewhere in the middle.

He said, "I spent forty years working for NASA as an engineer."

"Impressive. My wife's a scientist."

"You don't say?"

"A particle physicist."

He chuckled. "Ah, she wants to look into the eyes of God. I admire that. I just hope she realizes that God keeps his eyes shut most of the time."

"Well," I said. "She's got a crowbar."

Did he understand my metaphor? Do you understand it? I meant a particle accelerator, or whatever you use to observe the unobservable.

I asked, "So what brings you way up here?"

"I'm a consultant for polyurethane manufacturers. I'm giving a symposium in Forty Mile tomorrow afternoon on, well, preventative techniques to ward off mildew."

I drew my lips in. He continued, "Ever hear of the memory foam mattress?"

"Certainly."

"I invented it."

Now tell me, Elizabeth, was this chaos disguised as order, or was this a true synchronicity? Had memory foam not recently occupied my thoughts? And here was its Grand Creator, chatting with me in Canada. Maybe the Barnes & Noble books are right?

"That's so cool!" I said, failing to conceal my excitement. "I've been driving a lot. I have half a memory foam mattress in my trunk, but I slept on it outside, and now all these chunks of dirt and rocks are stuck in it."

Elroy shook my hand again. He liked shaking hands. "I brought along a lot of free samples for the symposium, and you're welcome to take a roll. It's a newer design, enhanced, non-combustible, and immediately kills pestering mites and mildew. As we say, 'Better sleep, better memories.'"

He told me the gift was in the back of his Pontiac, which was currently being fixed. He'd fallen asleep at the wheel early in the afternoon, and had jumped a curb at 25MPH, bending the axle. I said, "Asleep at the wheel? Do you have a sleep disorder?"

"Crazy, isn't it? I have insomnia. The truth is, I don't sleep on my inventions. Too superstitious, I guess."

"Superstitious about what?"

He bent closer. "We created memory foam to absorb high pressures in rocket takeoff, but then we found a more practical use, that is, as a mattress. When its marketability became obvious, well, I was having some personal issues, difficulty letting go of something in the past. See, I was sent on a bombing run in Cambodia. 1973. I didn't agree with the mission, but they told me it was necessary, and, should I die, it would be a most honorable death. Dying to free everyone else."

"So you went?"

"Oh, I went," he said. "My plane got shot down. They crucified me, those Cambodians. But that's irrelevant now. We're all free. The point is, when memory foam was developed for sleeping, I was struggling with my war memories. I slept on it for a month, and my dreams were, well, my unconscious was still in Cambodia, I guess. The powerful memories, provoked by the name of the very product I'd created, had seeped into my mind, had started to haunt me day in and day out. It was like the memory foam was saying 'Remember! Remember! Remember!' In order to let my past go, I needed to rid my life of all the suggestive symbols. The first thing to go was the memory foam. I adapted to hard surfaces. Nothing can enter my mind through a thick floorboard."

"Has it worked?"

"Not very well for sleeping," he said. "But no bad dreams."

Before I could continue the conversation, the door swung open and a mechanic entered. "Wally Tiparoy? Your car's ready."

Elroy stood. "You want that memory foam?"

I thought for a moment and considered that I should take after Elroy and sleep on the floor from now on. But I wasn't entirely willing to give up comfort for a clear conscience. I said, "Yes, I'd appreciate that very much."

A minute later, my arms were full of polyurethane.

Elroy whispered, "It was great meeting you. Don't be too hard on yourself, OK? It'll drive you crazy."

August 2

After staying the night at the Moonlight Inn, I ventured through the Yukon Territory. There was no snow, but it was close to zero degrees. The endless mountains were arranged like a washboard, the trees and lakes as enticing as stains on wood. As I sped through a valley, I thought about how, if you were here with me, you'd make a poetic comment about the dark, verdant hills disappearing into twilight's purple sky. You'd note all the frosty fir trees, the pines swinging in the wind. I hated having nobody to talk to. Your absence made nature so appalling, so unbearable. The more I thought about you, the more anxious I became about my trip's potential ramifications.

Have I screwed up? Maybe I've fallen for the notion that when people go on road trips, they change. Every year, shelves of memoirs on the matter get published, and thousands of films with one too many silent driving montages illuminate the screens in artsy movie houses, fooling folks like me into believing that motion is better than medicine. But what about the countless idiots who go on quests and end up fucking themselves? We don't ever hear about them.

I'm thinking about the first time I left, how, when you called me in Wisconsin, you said, "I don't understand why you always run away from the people who love you. You've got to run toward them. Wally, please, please turn around."

Elizabeth, this is difficult. Maybe it wasn't a good idea. I don't want to hurt you any more than I already have, but coming home right now would be just as pointless as continuing the journey. I'm too close to my destination to make a U-turn. What was I thinking? Nothing can come of a pilgrimage without a partner. Jim had Huck. Kerouac had Cassady. Lennie had George. Gulliver had no one. Look what happened to him.

The note I left on the shower curtain should have said:

Dear Elizabeth,

Let's just drop everything and drive as far north as we can go. The scenery and your company might purge me of my need to rely on medication and my connection to the past. You've always championed natural approaches, and I believe the time for reflection, combined with the distance from our busy lives in Cincinnati, might do wonders for us. I'm ready when you are.

Ah, that's my guilty conscience speaking. That's Satan whispering in my ear, as Becky would describe it. The truth is I'm changing—I'm changing a lot—and my ego, terrified of altering the status quo, is trying to convince me otherwise. I'm not going to listen. If I stop now, I'll never become the husband you've always wanted.

I'm writing from a town called Watson Lake. I'm no longer in a hurry. The cold weather has slowed my mind. At the Visitor's Center, the receptionist suggested I go ice fishing if I want to have the true Watson Lake experience. I only went fishing once, in the sixth grade, and like driving through the Yukon, it sucked. That same year, my parents were still gone and Grandpa was maniacal. As the abuse increased, my grades plummeted from excellent to atrocious. My teachers weren't suspicious; rather, Mr. Graw and Mrs. Mercer saw my academic deterioration as a sign of laziness.

Just south of the Visitor's Center is the Signpost Forest, which is a bunch of road signs nailed to posts. I wonder, if I go in there, will I come out feeling renewed?

When I was in sixth grade, my body became a signpost forest of its own. Aside from the terrible acne, I had bloated bags under my eyes from insomnia. My face was pale with terror but for cheeks that showed varying degrees of red, depending on the force of Grandpa Marvin's open palm. I was scared of the bullies beating me up at school and scared of being beat up at home. I carved a crucifix in my left bicep to remind me that, at the very least, my pain was trivial compared to Jesus' suffering on his own signpost.

I looked like a walking question mark, my posture taking the shape of my thoughts. Every day, I dragged my signpost forest around, hoping to find someone who would show me the way out. But the few people who came by simply said, "You're not working up to your potential."

The last time I prayed to God, I said, "You're not working up to your potential."

———————

My parents stayed in China for years. Aunt Eve never called them, as far as I know. Even if she had, what could they have done? They were political prisoners, and wouldn't be released from the Guizhou labor camp until they confessed the names of the revolutionaries who'd set fire to a building owned by the Chinese Catholic Patriotic Association. My parents trusted Grandpa because they believed in redemption. God had made them redeemers, after all. Years later, my father told me that while he and Mom worked in a factory in Guizhou, they'd converted half the criminals there. He said, "Fifty, maybe even a hundred, fates sealed, their names written in the book of eternity."

I saw things differently. Grandpa's change of heart in 1976 came about not because of a sincere admission of guilt and desire to repair damages, but because his liver had become enlarged. He was in the early stages of cirrhosis, and with Grandma having left him, with no friends or family or intricate system of guilt-prone enablers and caretakers, he feared his life would end slow and painfully. So he manipulated my parents, knowing that their Catholic ideals, their "God is love" view of the world, was their greatest vulnerability.

He faithfully adhered to his performance of a sinner seeking penance, despite the disparaging semi-annual biopsy results. Even with death's cold eyes fixed on him, Marvin stayed in character, not once uttering a foul word or slamming a door. No wonder everyone was convinced that Grandpa had transformed.

Maybe, to some degree, his alteration was legitimate. I studied theater arts. I took a class on performance theory, and both performance scholars and psychologists agree that sometimes we become the roles we play.

When Grandpa's liver had inexplicably renewed itself—an act of God's mercy, according to my parents—the devil was awakened. Nobody saw it that way, though. We were all blinded by the miracle. My parents interpreted the phenomenon as a divine message. God was telling them they need not worry about Molly and me being taken care of while they were in China.

While God prefers to murder every innocent baby in Egypt because of a blockheaded Pharaoh; while God rains down burning sulfur on two cities because of a few naughty perverts; while God uses a civilization-massacring flood for the purpose of scaring future generations into good behavior (why hadn't He just given Noah the Ten Commandments and spared his victims, rather than waiting 400 years before writing it all down?); Satan, on the other hand, understands the rewards of subtly. After Marvin had given me a peanut butter and Ajax sandwich, he backed off for a while. He even expressed a renewed interest in my intellectual and physical development. After three or four New York Yankees games and a trip to the Hayden Planetarium, I'd all but forgotten about that singular, horrible day (I did, however, internalize the possibility that my parents hadn't wanted me).

He dispensed his irreverence in a slow, controlled trickle. An incident here or there—like the time he'd dictated my wish-list for Santa, or another time, when he tied me up for twelve hours because I'd wandered into the woods behind the house—dispersed evenly throughout the years. Sometimes, when he'd drive me to pee-wee league baseball practice or to a friend's house, he'd slam the brakes and let my seatbelt do what his hands were at first reluctant to do. Then, months later, after the thrill of indirect abuse had worn off, he'd jab my leg with a safety pin he always carried. "That's for safety," he'd say. "Always be alert. You never know what's going to happen next." I endured the poking for years. By sixth grade, my legs and thighs were an astrological map of the universe's reddest stars, a constellation of just how unsafe I was. Sometimes I wished he wouldn't be so subtle, that he'd use a knife and just stab me in the thigh. Get it over with—one massive red supernova.

Jesus said that forgiveness is the only sane response. I believed in him at the time.

———————

At five o'clock, I went down to the Watson Lake Hotel bar and ordered a hamburger and fries. I took out my copy of *Why I Am Not a Christian*, but then, three college students approached me. One said, "Anyone who reads Bertrand Russell in a motel bar in Watson Lake has to be an American." His name was Phil. They were students at the University of Washington and had come here to visit Phil's sister. I told them that I, too, was a college student, studying theology at Cincinnati Christian University. "I'm on academic leave," I said. "I received a grant to study the Episcopalian Movement in the Yukon."

We ate together and swapped adventure stories, all of mine fabricated. Finally, Phil asked if I'd ever seen the northern lights. I told him I had, years ago in Vermont. "OK," he said, "but have you ever seen them stoned?"

———————

I'm high. On pot. No northern lights tonight, only interior lights. Being zooted makes me think of quantum physics, which makes me want to believe everything they say at Barnes & Noble is true. We create reality with our thoughts.

One night, while we were eating Indian takeout for dinner, you tried to explain renormalization in gravity physics. You said that if gravity were a particle rather than a field, all the gravity particles would attract each other. The collective force would become infinite. It would make existence impossible. In an effort to solve this dilemma, you conjectured that either a portion of our universe's gravity exists in other dimensions—that's why gravity is so weak—or space-time is actually a continuum, like a fluid; and the forces that govern physics present themselves as separate from each other, but are actually different characteristics of one thing. "Particles appear as particles, but they're really just a concept, a totality of interactions."

You were getting deep. I bit into my tasteless *mattar paneer*.

You said, "If space-time is woven together, that would account for particle substitutions. That would prove the existence of the B-Gravitrope and the gravitational force discrepancies."

I couldn't share your enthusiasm because I didn't know what you were talking about. But I wanted to know. You were just incapable of explaining it.

That weekend, I bought a book called *How to Survive in the Quantum Universe*. Then I bought another one called *Mind Matters: Understanding Self Through Quantum Physics*. I had left the second book by the toilet, and when you went to defecate, you found it there. You brought it into the living room and said, "What the hell is this?"

I shrugged. "I'm trying to learn about physics."

"This is misinformation! The author has no credibility! Why don't you just ask me if you have questions?"

"Because you're not good at explaining things."

This outraged you. You said, "No, you're not good at listening."

I huffed. You continued, "This stuff breeds stupidity."

Despite your beliefs, I felt brilliant when I read that garbage, and brainless every time you talked about physics. Whenever we sat down to talk, the conversation would inevitably go back to the B-Gravitrope. The fucking thing was hypothetical—you once said finding it was as unlikely as finding Santa Claus—but we talked about it as if it were a steel beam. You shrouded your insecurity with scientific rhetoric. I felt so miserably stupid.

Understand this, if you can: Soundwave was impractical.

My friends and family were unable to detect the urgency behind my need to own that toy because I lacked the rhetorical know-how to express it. As I got older and learned impressive words, I was still barred from communicating my desires because adults aren't supposed to want toys. Hell, I put Soundwave on our wedding gift registry. Yet everyone—including you—overlooked it, like it was a joke. What I should have done was offer an eloquent explanation, one that would make everyone feel so dumb that they'd buy me the toy just to make me shut up.

Elizabeth, let's not depreciate Soundwave's aesthetic supremacy; his form carries a greater significance than his function. Notice how the delicate contour of his royal blue casing encapsulates the industrial gray interior, suggesting the tensions between the natural and the mechanized. As Soundwave transforms from robot to object, he subordinates his higher function to a utilitarian ideology, and his box-like containment of self becomes indicative of repressed revolutionary desire. His inability to play cassettes shows that the prevailing ideology will not let him speak, yet his very being infers a direct relation to this oppressive ideology, and one must wonder if his inability to perform is identical to the worldview that created him. Is he aware of this defect? His consciousness is false, his true nature concealed within the illusion of function. His position in this terrain is that of an objectified commodity. He becomes alienated from his inner-world; his life no longer belongs to him, but to the object of his degrading transformation, an object of immense silence. Do you understand what the fuck I'm saying?

Had Santa respected my wishes, Soundwave would have prepared me to accept my own functional misgivings within the manufactured causality of the adult world. The toy would have taught me about use, rather than pleasure.

His name was Soundwave, yet he emitted no sound. His name described his limitation. A faucet that drips only when you're not listening to it. I thought that maybe if I had him, my grandfather, aunt, and sister would hear his silence and just stop.

They'd stop.

They'd be like that particle before you unlocked it from chaos. Not just my grandfather, but my mind, Elizabeth, my mind would seek a mutual state of coherency with Soundwave's inaudible existence, a tape player that played nothing but nothing.

Every week, I'd cut his picture out of the Toys "R" Us ads in the newspaper and send them to Santa. I once wrote, "Santa, please bring me this fucking piece of shit. I went a whole year without pulling my sister's hair. Do you hear me?"

In 1983, seven years old, I unwrapped the footballs, each stuffed in different sized boxes. I was so eager, starving, the excitement becoming anguish with the passing of each gift, the paper becoming Santa's flesh as I tore into him, pulling, severing, maiming cartilage, unhooking organs, dismantling him piece by piece, discarding skin so that I could get at what was inside.

After we listened to Christmas music and rested, Marvin ordered me to clean the mess of wrapping paper. My aunt and sister washed the dishes, and Bing Crosby's "Silent Night" played in the background at full volume. While I stuffed a Hefty bag with the wrapping paper, Grandpa seized my arm and squeezed it, ruptured some of the fresher pinholes. By this time, he'd moved on to poking my arms with the safety pin. His universe was expanding. Marvin's nose looked like a rotting apple, his narrow eyes compacted with abhorrence. His words were clotty, as if chunks of eggnog were stuck in his throat. He said, "Are you happy?"

"No," I said.

He snickered. "You wanted… what was it called, Sound Man?"

"Soundwave."

"Well, what did you do wrong this year?"

"Everything," I said, looking down at the three footballs Santa had given me. Footballs I'd eventually throw in the woods and leave there.

"That's right. Everything. And you should be glad we're not telling your father about all your crap, your outbursts at school. I still have friends in the sanitation business who would love to have a kid with your energy."

He lit a cigarette. "I know your dad still hates me for that, for making him work when he was a child. But this is different. *He was a victim.* And I shouldn't have victimized him. But you, well, you're a victim to your own self. If you work on a garbage truck, it's because you put yourself there."

"I'm too young to work on a garbage truck."

"Oh," he said, "there's always work to be done. The important thing is, you can't hate me for this. Now play with your footballs."

I knew he was bluffing. My father would kill him if he put me on a dump truck. But I also knew the dump truck meant something greater. Marvin would find a way to strip me of my childhood. He'd force me to become old and mean and, as a final product, I'd be Marvin. That was his goal: to replicate. To impose his genes on mine.

He sent me to my room and made sure I brought the footballs with me. I looked at my three other Transformer toys, which I'd put on top of my two-tier bookshelf. Earlier that morning, I'd moved them over to make space for Soundwave.

But that wasn't all I'd done. I'd made the bed in my parents' room. I'd fished out Dad's pipe tobacco from a cabinet in the basement and put it on the table next to the recliner that he used to lounge in while watching baseball. I found back-issues of *Good Housekeeping* and stuffed them into the magazine basket beside Mom's recliner. I pulled out Marvin's *Car and Driver* and *Golf Week* magazines, and tossed them in the trash.

God had given Marvin a new liver in order to show my parents that He approved of their intention to go to China. Likewise, I believed that Soundwave signified Santa's assurance that Mom and Dad would come back.

Three footballs.

August 3

I'm in Dawson, late afternoon, at Klondike Kate's Restaurant. From this point on, Route 5 will bring me into the Arctic Circle. My Mapquest directions warned me of "portions unpaved." I wonder if maybe the Honda will give up, being that it's 1,000 miles past due on an oil change. I've had the heat cranked, but lately it's failed to thaw the windows. And the car has been shaking much more than usual.

I imagine that everyone in Dawson feels powerless. With so much unyielding earth surrounding you, it'd be impossible to have a superiority complex. In Cincinnati, we've resolved the nature-versus-man dilemma by erecting strip malls and high-rise apartments, which obscure our view of the earth beyond. As far as we're concerned, nothing will outlive us. Of human triviality, we know zilch. Every ten years, one store replaces another in a ceaseless, conveyor-belt-like motion, as if the point of urban renewal is to prevent the horizon from leaking in. By contrast, in the Yukon, the signs of human impermanence are everywhere. It must make people feel so cautious.

Most of Dawson's buildings look deliberately old-fashioned, indicating that the town takes pride in conserving its gold-rush-era architecture. Or they need tourists. I'd venture to say the latter, only because of the bombastic, multi-colored ways in which Dawson's road signs embellish what would otherwise be the most trivial attractions. There's the Jack London Shack, the Dredge Number Four Historical Site, and Dogsled Park.

Klondike Kate had called out sick. This was not a surprise, given the town's average August temperature of 23 degrees. From the outside, the restaurant looks stuck in time, a relic of 1898, when the lust for gold inspired people to scour the creeks and ravish the hillsides. The building's shape is boxy, creamy banana yellow, its awnings modest in comparison to the eye-stabbing architecture in Cincinnati. Old jars line the windowsill, and the menu items are hand-painted in generous, neon strokes on a crooked corkwood sign. The interior, however, reminds me of T.G.I. Friday's. Slanted photographs and paintings fill the walls: Charlie Chaplin, a Ragtime band, a dogsled team of bearded men smoking pipes. A rusty pair of skates hangs over a horizontal support beam.

———————

Elizabeth, why did I leave? I'm beginning to wonder if this journey is making me more like Marvin. I fear that it's somehow augmenting the Marvin gene rather than exterminating it. Was he not a man of impulse, a man who'd immediately react to emotional stimuli, often in ways that would hurt others? Was he not completely devoid of empathy?

I'm so damn far from everything that I can't even tell who I am anymore. Hell, out here, not even the memory foam can remember what it is and where it belongs. I rolled it into a ball, and now it's stuck that way, enclosed within itself.

All of this reminiscing on Marvin has churned up memories of sixth grade. See, that year, my peers decided I was an awkward dweeb, deserving of frequent backhanded slaps to the head. I don't blame them. I surely had it coming. I wore outdated clothes consisting of bright green sweatpants and striped shirts with collars that reached over my shoulders. My face was caked with zits. If someone had been smart enough to squeeze my head in a vice, he'd have solved the oil crisis for at least another twenty years.

After enduring bullies all day, I'd get off the school bus at 3PM. There were no sighs of relief. Marvin would be waiting by the door, hands on his hips. Sometimes, he'd have the safety pin ready, concealed in his palm. Other times, he'd make me an afternoon snack. Ham and litter-box-dust sandwiches. Chicken tenders with a light coating of Ajax, barely noticeable to the eye, but progressively fatal for my stomach lining. He sometimes heated up a bowl of Chunky Soup, and dotted the surface with scraps of aluminum foil. I had cavities, and if you've ever chewed aluminum foil after dental work, you'd know that it'd be less painful to bite a hornet's nest. Finally—and I can't be quite sure about this—I think he once served me roadkill. Whatever the beast was—a squirrel, a rabbit, a possum—it was hairy and tasted like it had been rotting for a few days. At least he had the decency to cook it a little. He didn't want me to die, after all.

If I refused to eat his toxic concoctions, I wouldn't get any meals. Sometimes, Aunt Eve would bring me a dish in the middle of the night and mumble some justification: "He's just trying to shape you into a man." But those times were infrequent; she generally attended to Molly and kept out of the grandfather-grandson drama.

Molly once put a few McDonald's hamburgers in her backpack and snuck them down to my room. She hadn't considered Marvin's primitive knack for sniffing out meat; he could smell a steak thrown on a grill as far away as Indiana. He intercepted Molly, dragged her by the hair to her bedroom and, I suppose mercifully, smacked her around.

By December of sixth grade, I weighed seventy-three pounds. Nobody, not a single person, pulled me aside and said, "Wally, is everything OK? You don't look well."

I recall a book report I wrote that year. It was about child abuse. I got a C. You know how many times I've re-read that thing? Whenever I flirt with being optimistic about the human race, I dig up this paper and remind myself that people are terrible. Granted, it was horribly written, but I'm shocked that my teacher failed to recognize it as a cry for help. I'd listed all the warning signs of abuse, the typical behaviors and gestures. I'd described myself in detail. Then I wrote: *Parents are not the only people who abuse children. Sometimes it's other relatives, like grandpas.* I argued that family members and teachers are often reluctant to intervene because they don't want to get personally involved. As an assurance, I wrote: *You cannot be sued for reporting abuse.* The kicker: at the end of the essay, I included the 800-number for the National Child Abuse Hotline.

That was the best I could do, Elizabeth. Early on, I had learned to hide things.

———

Although Dawson's Eldorado Hotel is a bit out of our price range, my options were limited. The hostel looked creepy, the Downtown Hotel was undergoing renovation, and the Aurora Inn was fully booked but for a single Jacuzzi suite. At least I'm getting what I pay for: I'm sitting in an ergonomic leather chair at a spacious mahogany desk. It's early evening, and had I lacked caution, I might be perusing the Jack London Interpretive Museum or attending the senior citizen's production of *Oedipus the King* at the Klondike Institute of Arts and Culture. Unfortunately, I had an incident earlier, and it's probably in my best interest to stay indoors now.

Several hours ago, I was writing you from Klondike Kate's. After two cups of coffee, I felt like a different beverage for a change. While the lone waiter/cook boiled water for my hot chocolate, I looked out the front window toward the pine-covered mountains that encircled the town.

There was one other man in the restaurant; he'd been there the entire time. His jacket read, "Dawson Fire Company." He was eating eggs and sausage and doing a crossword puzzle. He looked strikingly like my father, his face a wrinkled oval but his nose sharp, his cheeks bloodless and eyes permanently troubled. Had I been standing at a distance, I would have thought he was Dad.

My father's life was a progression from dump truck to fire truck. He disposed of what was dead and then rescued the living. I wanted to be like him, but he was gone. God took him. One little car accident and my parents were obliterated. When I was twenty, I would rather have had God send my parents to China. Instead, he sent them to the afterlife.

The cook brought the mug of hot chocolate to my table. She said, "Is this your first time in Dawson?" She untied her apron and laid it over the counter, as if I would be the last customer of the day.

"Uh-huh. I live in Ohio, but I'm originally from New York."

The fireman glanced over his crossword puzzle at me.

She said, "This is a nice place, very homely."

"I like the architecture." There was too much artificial sweetener in the hot chocolate. It tasted like rubber bands.

"What brings you to Dawson?"

I told her I was a geneticist. I rattled off my sister's credentials, but attributed them to myself. "I'm giving a lecture up in Inuvik. On biological-emotional determinism."

The fireman put down his crossword puzzle. "What's that?" he said.

"It's the heredity of emotional states. Like, for instance, say your father was a happy man but prone to indecision—"

"That's not how he was," said the fireman.

"Right. I'm just being hypothetical. Anyway, I've been looking for the kind of gene that would predispose you to your father's indecision—"

The fireman said, "I'm not indecisive. And like I said, neither was he."

"I'm not saying that you, or anyone, is indecisive—"

"Then quit saying 'you.'"

The cook said, "Benny, don't start having a temper tantrum again. I told you that you're not welcome here if you have another blowout." She turned to me. "Couple of weeks ago, a group of gentlemen came up here and—"

Benny pointed at her. "They were all minority thugs."

"They were American hip-hop musicians, Benny." She smiled at me apologetically.

Benny said to me, "Those *people* were filming a rap video. Called it 'She's Freezing My Nuts Off.'" He glared at the cook. "You just wait, Marcy. You know how Americans are. Two weeks from now, we'll start seeing truckloads of them, those so-called hip-hop types. It'll become a fad. They'll all start rapping about being cold, and they'll keep coming back here."

Marcy said, "It'd be good for business."

He laughed. "You mean it'll be good for insurance companies who cover theft." He looked at me. "You're an American. You tell me, what are they like where you live? Wait! Before you answer that, you say you're a genetic scientist, right?"

"Yes." I wanted to leave right then.

"And you specialize in, what do you call it?"

I couldn't remember what I'd said. I quickly made up a scientific term. "Biogenetic Autogenous Affectation. BAA for short."

"Fine, whatever you call it. Let's assume that you're right. A person's emotions are handed down. Father to son, or whatever. And let's say that robbing houses and dealing drugs comes from having immoral emotions. This means, if I'm correct, that most black people suffer from BAA, right? Isn't something like forty-percent of them in jail?"

Marcy looked at me inquisitively.

I said, "Um." I sipped my hot chocolate and gagged. "There are a lot of factors involved, like poverty and the trappings of capitalism—"

"But the truth is, even if they were all rich, they'd still act like beasts because they have BAA."

Without thinking much about the consequences, I said, "No doubt, certain attitudes might be hereditary. Was your father a racist?"

He cleared his throat, leaned back, stretched his legs under the table, and rounded his shoulders. He said, "Was your father a liar?"

"Excuse me?"

"You're no genetic scientist. You think I'm stupid?"

I wondered how he'd figured me out. As far as I could tell, I'd delivered a flawless performance. I said, "You're terribly mistaken."

"Let me ask you something. Who's the father of modern genetics?"

Now I was screwed. He'd asked me to provide the most basic snippet of textbook knowledge, and I felt stumped. Take a guess at what grade I was in when we first learned about genetics. Sixth grade, Elizabeth. I hadn't absorbed anything that year. Then, in high school, I was such an academic dumbass that I didn't have to take Biology. I'd taken a "special" class called Earthquakes and Volcanoes. As a theater major in college, my science electives were Food Chemistry and The Weather And You. Listen, I'm not going to blame all of my ignorance on academic institutions; I was partially accountable. I'd never once checked out a biology book from the library, or walked across our living room and plucked one of your general science books from the shelf. As far as I was concerned, Molly had that area covered. There was no incentive for me to understand genetics because, in my mind, biology meant Molly's success and, by virtue of sibling rivalry, my failure.

So who's the father of genetics? I'd recalled the day when Mr. Graw brought a bunch of plants to class. He'd lined them up on a table. But what the hell did he say? I was preoccupied that day; I had a Van Halen song stuck in my head. It was "Girl Gone Bad," from the album *1984*, and it had been rolling around my mind for a week. And then, to further impair my concentration, Kim Emberly sat nearby, wearing shorts for the first time that year, her golden legs swinging as Mr. Graw lectured, her adorable feet barely touching the floor.

She'd slipped me a note that said: *Stop looking at me. Every time you look at me, other people notice and it makes me feel lame and retarded.*

I had an archive of similar notes at home, but this one was particularly painful. She'd never barred me from flicking glances at her before. In that moment, the last thing I cared about was a lesson on some ancient plant collector's discovery.

"Well?" said Benny.

I knew the scientist's name had an M at the beginning. That much I could recall. The next letter had to be a vowel, so I ran through them: Ma...Me... Yes, it was an E. I could almost hear the name in my mind. It was Meh-something. I said, "Mendelssohn."

Benny raised an eyebrow. "Really?"

"Yes."

"Mendelssohn was a classical music composer."

Marcy sighed. She turned her back and busied her hands, shuffling the bags of coffee beans on display.

Benny said, "For your information, it's Mendel. You were close—"

I said, "My memory gets cluttered when I'm on the spot."

"I'm sure it does. See, I've been doing a crossword puzzle a day for over twenty years. I'm not stupid. Now what I want to know is, why are you lying?"

Great question. I felt tempted to make up some more bullshit. I could have told him I was a researcher, conducting social experiments on people's willingness to believe stories they hear from total strangers. But I sensed that if I took this any further, he'd bash a chair over my head.

I settled for honesty. "I'm lying because I've got nothing to lose. You don't know me, we'll probably never meet again, so maybe a little recklessness is OK. I've been traveling for days, and I need to, you know, entertain myself however I can."

His skin tightened. He wanted to get up, but he fought the impulse. "Recklessness isn't OK in this town. I don't know if *you've* got some kind of genetic problem, like you're bipolar or something, but you're lucky that Marcy and I have this little no-violence agreement. Otherwise, I'd take you out back and break your fucking hands. So be careful about what you say, punk."

Marcy said, "Benny's right. I don't know who you think you are, but that's not the way we communicate around here."

Benny glared at me, waiting for a response. I could see his crossword puzzle on the table, almost complete but for one row. I said I was sorry.

He waved at me dismissively and turned his head away. He picked up his pencil and looked down at the crossword puzzle.

Marcy said, "You finished?" She held her hand out.

I looked into my mug. It was half full.

"Yeah, I'm finished." I gave her the mug and placed four, one-dollar Canadian coins on the countertop. I was going to make for the door and just leave this embarrassing experience behind, but I felt like I needed to alleviate the awkwardness. I wanted closure.

Benny was still laboring over that one word, holding his pencil upside down and tapping the eraser on the table. "What's the question?" I said.

He looked up at me. "Huh?"

I pointed at the crossword puzzle.

"You serious?" he said.

"Yes."

"Christ, you're stubborn." He glanced down at the crossword puzzle and read, "Shakespeare's early tragedy, *Titus* blank. Ten letters. Third one is a D, and the last one is an S."

This, Elizabeth, was a synchronicity. Another one for my list. I said, "*Titus Andronicus!*"

He looked at the row. He was mentally stamping the letters into their boxes. He turned his pencil over and scribbled the letters in. Then, he sat back and stared at the completed puzzle.

I said, "It's a strange play. Unlike Shakespeare's others because it's so violent. Revenge plays were popular back then, so I guess Shakespeare was just trying to keep up with the times."

Benny rubbed his chin. "You a thespian or something?"

"A playwright, to be specific."

"Good thing you're not an actor. You wouldn't get too far."

"Right," I said, motioning toward the door. "Good luck with your crossword puzzles, and putting out fires."

"Oh," he said, tugging on his jacket. "I'm no fireman. This is my brother's."

"I see," I said, turning the doorknob.

As the cold air rushed inside, Benny said one more thing. "I don't know if you're really going to Inuvik or not, but—"

"I am."

"Then be careful. You might think it's easy to fuck with people's heads in Dawson, but up in Inuvik, they won't think twice about throwing you in the Arctic Ocean."

I wouldn't allow myself to wallow in remorse. There was a bright side to this experience: I'd witnessed a synchronicity. The universe had left an empty row on Benny's crossword puzzle just for me. What is the likelihood that a former theater major, who had recently browsed Kyle's book on Shakespeare, would walk into Benny's life just as he was struggling to answer a question about Shakespeare? Furthermore, *Titus Andronicus* is an obscure play—so obscure, in fact, that it's the only one I've read from beginning to end. It's about revenge, a topic that has always fascinated me because it's practical.

I dabbled in revenge when I was a teenager, though never without moderation and caution. I was particularly adept at an early form of hacking called phreaking. It meant "phone hacking." Whenever a jock knocked me on my ass during school, I'd get back by fucking up his family's telephone service. They might pick up their landline and hear an unexpected though familiar-sounding recording of an operator saying, "Please deposit twenty-five cents to make this call." They might wonder why, out of nowhere, hundreds of calls made to a law office in Tacoma, Washington were being forwarded to their home. Given my troubles with interpersonal communications, it's no wonder I'd become fascinated with phreaking. I felt control.

Not all of my vengeance happened from a distance. I'd developed my stealth skills after a few years of sneaking into the girls' locker room whenever Kim was in gym class. By eighth grade, I'd basked in the scent of her garments a hundred times, never once getting caught. Granted, secretly sniffing a girl's underwear, training bra, and socks is hardly revenge, but in my mind, these clandestine offenses balanced the karmic scales.

With Marvin, payback came in controlled increments. I was, in effect, mirroring his carefully timed delivery of abuses. I'd pluck dollar bills from his wallet, put spiders in his underwear drawer, sprinkle pepper into his instant coffee jar. None of these minor infractions were fulfilling. I knew that, sooner or later, I'd have to do something massive. He deserved it. The fucker had ruined me: I had an eating disorder, and I was doomed to cover my legs for the rest of my life because of all the pin holes. I nurtured the desire to engage in full retaliation. I delayed as long as I could, waiting for the day when Marvin would be too old and weak to fight back.

By the time I reached high school, my parents were done evangelizing China. The Chinese government, in an effort to appease the increasing number of citizens who'd become infected by the "Christian fever," recognized the Open Church, which was state-regulated Catholicism. Although the change in policy was hardly a victory—most regarded it as a crafty way for the regime to keep track of Catholics—the church was now permitted to affiliate with Rome and consent to papal primacy. Consequently, a number of prisoners—all Americans—were released.

Although I'd love to provide you an in-depth exposition of how I handled my parents' return—the rough transition, my struggle to extinguish the resentment that boiled in me— there are more important concerns.

Now that Mom and Dad were home, the question was what to do with Grandpa. We didn't have enough room in the house for him. He didn't want to live in a retirement community; he wanted his own condo. His health—but for a smoker's cough—was excellent. So long as he took his liver medication, he maintained his vigorous condition and, therefore, assisted living would have been a waste of money. After days of debating, he bought a condo in New Jersey, only a half-hour drive away.

During high school, I had exhibited a lot of "antisocial behaviors." That's the term that the school psychologist used. The police regularly knocked on our door because I'd broken someone's windows or shoplifted Nintendo games from Toys "R" Us. After I'd spent three Saturdays doing work detail—washing ambulances and police cars—I wanted to know what was wrong with me, why I felt compelled to do bad things. It was the first time I wondered if I had inherited Marvin's wickedness. It was the first time I wished to find evidence that I'd acquired all of my characteristics and dispositions from my mother's side of the family, rather than my father's. I wanted to discover proof that my genetic code was primarily linked to the preferable, if not morally virtuous, Prynne-Donovan-Southpaw identity, that my nature was aligned with the Prynnes, but I'd been nurtured into being a Tiparoy.

Of course, there was no way to find out. The best I could do was to make an effort to correct my bad behaviors. In order to do that, I needed to equip myself with knowledge. I went to the school library and took out books on psychology and self-help.

According to *Post Traumatic Responses* by Dr. Randy Gillman, I was a problem-child because I had unfulfilled revenge fantasies. When a victimized child's desire to resist abuse is left unsatisfied, his personality becomes fragmented and he goes nuts. The book recommended psychoanalysis and, in some cases, medication.

Gillman suggested a form of therapeutic intervention in which the counselor guides the victim through an imagined revenge scenario. I wondered why the patient should even bother with a simulation when he could do the real thing. Artificial means produce artificial results. I decided I'd skip over the simulation and engage in an actual retributive act. I'd been waiting a long time to get back, after all.

One day, Dad sent me to Marvin's to drop off a box of mail-order vitamins and medications. I entered the house and walked through the living room, calling his name, and heard nothing but the TV. I put the box on the kitchen table and headed to the TV room. Marvin was on the recliner, smoking a cigarette and watching reruns of Gunsmoke. He tilted his head toward me. "Cut your hair. You look like a fag."

I stood in the doorway and said, "It's the grunge look. The good old days are over, Marv."

"Not if I have any say. So, what did you bring me?"

"I was supposed to bring you pills."

"Supposed to? Where are they?"

I took my backpack off and laid it at my feet. "I saw you're taking Lortab. That's a powerful narcotic, not something a doctor should prescribe to a man your age, especially when you have breathing difficulty. I read the label. I didn't bring your pills. They're compromising your safety."

"You're a doctor now? Wonderful."

"When I was a child, I wanted to be a doctor."

"And you're just as much a shit-for-brains now as you were then."

"That means nothing to me coming from a wrinkly old fuck."

He held his gaze on me for a moment, then took a fast drag of his cigarette. He spoke with an exhale, "The fruit doesn't fall far from the tree. Remember that, Wally. Remember it for the rest of your life. Sure, it might skip a generation. Might appear like that's all over now, like the bad people are no longer part of the family and never will be again because it's all been weeded out. Your dad became a good man, I'll give you that. But don't ever think you're like him, because you're not. You're more like me than anyone. I see it all over you."

"Is that why you've always hated me?"

He said, "I'll have your mother bring the pills over if it bothers you. So cut the crap. Go do your homework or something."

He looked back at the TV. My revenge wasn't working. I'd wanted him to panic.

I squatted in front of him so we could be eye to eye. The way his lashes fluttered, the way his pupils followed the trail of cigarette smoke instead of my intense stare, indicated anxious suspicion. He pressed his tongue against his teeth, then, finally meeting my eyes, he said, "What the hell has gotten into you?"

"Grandpa, why do you hurt people?"

He waved. "Get out of my face. What's wrong with you? Your mother, she made you a pussy. Go harass someone else. I'm an old man."

I raised my voice. "Why do you hurt people? Why do you act like you're reformed?"

He tried to look over my shoulder at the TV. I grabbed the remote and shut it off. A few years earlier he would have leapt up and strangled me, but as he grew older his atmosphere's escape velocity increased. Now, he heaved himself against gravity's restrictions. He was half bent, knees shaking, and I pressed my palm against his chest and pushed him back. He collapsed into the chair and pounded his fist on the armrest. The veins in his face hardened.

I said, "It sucks being vulnerable, doesn't it? Here's what I'm going to do. I'll tell Mom that I'll bring your dinner from now on. But I won't bring it. I'll eat it. I need to gain some weight, anyway. I'm still feeling a little starved from all those years you served me poison or nothing at all."

"Screw off. That'll never work."

"To make a case for your dementia, I'll say that you keep throwing the food in the garbage because you see bugs on it. I'll be right because I'm young, and you'll be wrong because you're old. And every time you want a drink, you'll have to be careful, because you'll never know which bottle contains a few drops of Clorox. The apple juice? Orange juice? Milk?"

"I'll have your parents and the police here in a minute." He laughed.

"And just so you don't forget to check your drinks before consuming them, I'll jab your leg with a safety pin."

"I can't feel anything in my legs anyway. Who do you think you are?"

"I can come here every day and strip you of enjoying your elderly years. Piss on your furniture and blame it on you. Shit in your bathtub and say, 'Look, he needs to be locked up!'"

"You're the one who needs to be locked up," he said. "Now go home."

I clutched his leg and squeezed my fingers into them. For the first time in my life, I saw fright in his eyes. I said, "The fruit doesn't fall far from the tree."

I grabbed his throat. His Adam's apple swelled in my palm. He didn't move. I pulled a safety pin from my front pocket and slowly brought its tip toward his right eye. He whimpered and mumbled, "No. Don't."

I said, "Now listen…" I inched it closer to his quivering pupil. "You've ruined lives. I don't want to hear an apology. That's just words."

He tried to speak but couldn't.

I said, "Don't worry, Grandpa, you're safe. This is just a simulation."

I drove the pin into his thigh. He shrieked; his arms shot out and his fingers stretched. His cry sounded like mine the first time he stabbed me. I drove it in again, five, six times, dots of blood staining his beige khaki pants, the noise like popping bubble wrap. After one last jab, I threw the pin into his lap and stared at him.

Marvin produced a wheeze. A dark spot expanded from his groin.

"Looks like you need a towel," I said.

His throat palpitated and he made a gargling sound. Frustrated, he shaped his lips around the words he wished to speak, as if that might let loose the hindered sounds. All I heard was the rumbling phlegm in his throat and a hiss of air. Marvin gave up and shook his head in defiance.

"No, I insist," I said, reaching for the backpack. "Oh, it looks like I didn't bring any towels, but don't fret. I brought you these." I unzipped the backpack and removed three footballs, lobbing them one by one into his wet lap. Then I headed for the door.

I said, "I'll have Mom bring you the pills. And the next time I come, I'll try to remember to bring you some diapers. I've got a feeling you're going to be pissing yourself a lot more, now that your body's breaking down. Anyway, if you need anything else from me, don't hesitate to call. We're family, right?"

———————

Am I supposed to tell you how much I regret doing that, Elizabeth? I don't feel any shame at all. I never have.

Jesus said that forgiveness is the only sane response. I say that at some point during his life, Jesus had lost touch with reality.

Here's a synchronicity: Two weeks after my revenge, Marvin fell asleep in bed with a cigarette in his hand. He had a combustible memory foam mattress. My father received the call from an old NYFD friend now stationed in Bergen County. By the time Dad arrived, half the condominium was consumed. My father stood on the lawn with the neighbors. There was nothing he could do. This was one of the many fires he couldn't stop.

Smoke inhalation got Marvin first. He was a dry log thrown into a bonfire; he cracked open, and all the flames and smoke from hell erupted from within him. The only remaining parts were his bones, teeth, and a stubborn cigarette butt. The polyurethane from the memory foam had melted into a sticky plastic that encapsulated his bones. I imagined that as it burned, it rolled in on itself and Marvin like a scorching cocoon.

August 4

I've made it to Fort McPherson, but I'm in terrible shape, physically and mentally. The drive took thirteen hours. I'm at the Fort McPherson Traveler's Lodge tonight. A brochure on the nightstand says, "Please Visit the Fort McPherson Tent & Canvas Factory." I'm not enticed. Nothing's enticing now. I just want to get to Inuvik. It's about 120 miles away, which up here could mean a five-hour drive.

My room's window looks out at snow. There's an amber light attached to the side of the motel, pointed at the ground. It's making the snow orange, a Martian landscape. There's a bookshelf in the room with *Pickwick Papers* between *Sir Gawain and the Green Knight* and *The Kite Runner*. Centuries merge in the grime. But at the shelf's far right, there's open space. Either they don't have enough books or someone has taken what was there. I hope to one day write something that could fill that space.

Once, I submitted a one-act play called *The 1994 Cigar* to The Midwest Association of Young Playwrights Annual New Voices in Drama Contest. A screener had scribbled a comment in my rejection letter's margin: "Not exactly the kind of play that would resonate with *anyone*. Zero awareness or consideration of audience."

Relatives on my mother's side of the family had also been afflicted with the literary bug. Christopher Donovan's

1896 novel, *The Water District*, received favorable reviews. It was about a community that had been devastated by the construction of Lake Cochituate—the reservoir that served Boston until 1951. It was Christopher's first and only novel, but he'd served as the *Brockton Beagle* newspaper's senior editor for two decades. Then there's Aunt Martha. She tried for years to get her novel, *77th Street*, published. It was about growing up as a Republican in Manhattan in the late 1950s and early 1960s, and what it was like not to be a beatnik. Publishers wouldn't take her seriously, but when she graduated from Columbia with a PhD in British Literature and wrote *John Donne: Poetics and the Art of Circular Reasoning*, literary critics praised her. Her follow-up was a modern translation of Peter Prynne's journals, the book that brought my parents together, the book that exemplifies all of my ideals.

For instance, on September 2, 1643, Peter Prynne wrote: *The sky is unpleasant today. I will attend to young Jane. I have eaten three more apples.*

On February 8, 1644, the day after he survived the gallows, he wrote: *The noose snapped twice. Jane and Henry smuggled me out by carriage. The sky is unpleasant today. I have eaten one apple, and obtained the promissory notes from Alfred.*

We could only guess what he was feeling, if he felt at all. It seemed like he was just playing along, unaware. So unimpressed that not even a noose could evoke passion.

Sometimes, I wondered if Peter Prynne had any personal, hereditary afflictions. There's no evidence in his journals that he might have drank too much, suffered from depression and anxiety, or had temper tantrums. But you can never trust a minimalist. It turned out that Peter did have a biological burden.

A year before you and I met, Aunt Martha let me view the Prynne and Donovan family archives at the Hoboken Community College library. As I read through her proofs of Prynne's journals, I realized that she'd omitted from the published version Peter's references to insomnia. I asked why.

"These journals," she said, "are meant to illuminate the political history of the English Civil War. For the sake of brevity and maintaining focus, I had to exclude Peter's domestic concerns."

I don't remember the dates of his musings about sleeplessness; I can't even give you a general idea of where they were situated on his timeline. Before the first hanging or after? Before his son's accident or after? I should have taken notes.

Nonetheless, he'd written something along the lines of *I'd rather be cursed with a lame leg than this lifelong restlessness.* More frequently, though, he quoted the Bible. He mimicked Job: *Night drags on and I am sated with tossings till morning twilight,* and David's pleas in Psalms: *I call on God to mind, I moan, I complain, my spirit fails. You have held my eyelids open.*

I can see you raising your right eyebrow. You're thinking, "Did Wally recite that from memory?"

Nope, but I wish I had the ability to drop Bible quotes at will. The Gideons, it seems, anticipated that someone, someday, might have a redemptive moment at the Fort McPherson Traveler's Lodge.

My discovery of Peter's insomnia was good news. Relatives on my father's side didn't have sleep disorders. The wicked were well rested. Yet, here was some proof that I'd inherited a Prynne-Donovan quality. If I could find another ten to twenty similarities, I'd be able to say, with certainty, that my genetic blueprint was modeled around a more favorable set of traits.

I'd cease living in fear of being locked into Marvin-endowed hereditary determinism. No reasonable insomniac would celebrate his ailment, of course. My finding was a victory, but it didn't offset my twenty-one years of accumulated, nocturnal despair. The bedtime anarchy continued. Sleep approached me every night with her usual reluctance, sometimes not at all.

That brings me to right now. I can't sleep. Should you one day write a biography of Wally Tiparoy, would you, like Aunt Martha, consider my meditations on restlessness so trivial that they need not be included? I'm amazed at the ease with which one who hasn't suffered can cast aside another's narrative of anguish.

From the moment my mother released me from her womb, I was a certified insomniac. Most days, I slept only a few hours, but certainly I needed more sleep. I cried ceaselessly, day and night, and my parents brought me to every doctor and specialist in a twenty-mile radius. Apparently, there was nothing wrong with me physically. Unsure what to do next, my parents considered bringing me to a priest to determine if I was possessed. Finally, once I'd learned enough words, I was able to provide a simple explanation for my wailings: "I'm so tired, but I can't sleep." We tried warm milk, increased activity during the day, relaxation exercises, and Herman Melville. Every night before bed, Dad would read me long passages from *Moby Dick*, all those musings on cetology and whaling boat management. I remained awake. We moved on to Boswell's *Life of Samuel Johnson*, Bunyan's *The Pilgrim's Progress*, and finally, *Why I Am Not a Christian* by Bertrand Russell. Dad would contest Russell's statements sentence by sentence, using the Bible and the writings of Thomas Aquinas and St. Francis to clarify God's illogical ways. I remained miserably awake and educated. Not long after my parents left, Marvin started giving me a shot of Benadryl every night. Then, as my tolerance developed, he'd increase the dosage. I moved on to Nyquil in seventh grade; and then, after my parents returned, after I started seeing a psychologist, I surveyed the world's benzodiazepine catalog. Each new medication would relieve my sleep disorder briefly, but ultimately it was hopeless. Until the FDA approved Ambien. I've no doubt you remember those three blissful months. I've also no doubt you remember when I came home from Dr. Dillman's office one day, distressed because he wouldn't refill my prescription. "It's for short term use," he'd said. "No doctor is going to take a liability risk by keeping you on Ambien indefinitely."

What baffled me was that you agreed. You said, "Well, it does say on the bottle that Ambien may be habit forming." I would hardly call sleep a habit. It's a luxury, but I shouldn't expect anyone who hasn't experienced the hell of never sleeping to understand.

Let's imagine that God was less merciful when He created you. Instead of doling out modest shortcomings in equal proportions among women of your design, He deposited a surplus of defects in you. The most unfavorable characteristic you'd received in this transaction was an overactive mind. Restlessness is the inevitable repercussion.

Re-imagine your life story. Start with a generic childhood recollection. Maybe one of those lazy winter evenings when your family would sit around the woodstove and Grandpa Stoll would read aloud from *Lord of the Rings*. Now, remove from your memory those contented yawns you emitted, the kind that resolved into cute, embarrassed grins. Instead, I want you to envision yourself grinding your teeth, picking at your cuticles, unable to get comfortable. I want you to miss entire pages of Grandpa Stoll's reading because you're preoccupied with your own discomfort. You think about your hips. Are they misshapen? Are the bones unnaturally malleable? Should you tell someone, or keep it to yourself? What if you're crippled? What if you have a disease? Maybe you should drink more milk. No, you think. It's not me. It's the floor. Why are there only two recliners in the living room? Why does Grandpa hog the entire couch? Children always have to sit on the floor. The misapprehension here is that children are exempt from pinched nerves, and pins and needles.

Picture everyone in the living room rising, your grandfather slipping a peacock feather between the book's pages and declaring, "To be continued tomorrow!" Hear everyone yawn. Watch yourself kissing your mother, father, grandfather, and brother on their cheeks. Listen to your voice say, "Goodnight." Notice how, now that we're revising your childhood, your voice has lost its sweet and jovial timbre. Hear it trail away. Detect its weariness. It knows what's coming next: an agonizing night of insomnia.

Watch your parents head upstairs to their bedroom. Feel the cold air roll inside as Grandpa departs. Listen as your brother flushes the toilet, washes his hands, says goodnight one more time, then closes his bedroom door. All is quiet but for the embers crackling in the woodstove. See the quilts and blankets left bundled on the recliners and couch. Walk reluctantly to your bedroom.

It's like being whipped. You're tied to the bed. The shadows are alive and thrashing you. You're sweating, but the damp sheets make you cold. You try to anesthetize yourself by thinking about happy things. You envision yourself as Dorothy.

You're dancing with the Scarecrow. But soon, a thought pops into your mind: *I'm thinking about something happy.* You follow that thought. You think about how you're trying to think about pleasurable situations, how you've succeeded, and the result of this awareness is yet another thought: *I'm no longer thinking about something pleasurable.*

You center yourself. You focus. The process repeats itself, again and again.

It's 1:30AM. You will be tired tomorrow. You'll have no energy. You think, *This is ruining my life! God, please, I beg you, let me sleep!*

2:00AM.

2:45AM.

2:46AM.

He won't help you, Elizabeth. He gave that gift to someone else.

So do you give up? Do you get out of bed? Or do you stay there, determined to outwit God's design?

———

The alarm clock on the nightstand has blue digits instead of red. It's 4:06AM. This is the second time tonight that I've gotten up, turned on the light, and did something else. Honestly, the last thing I want to be doing right now is writing you. Nothing personal. I'm just not feeling as fluid as I did in Dawson, or at that truck stop in North Dakota. The TV only picks up local channels, and the one program that's not mostly shrouded in static is a French sitcom.

Earlier, during the first round of tonight's insomnia, I thought about finding a CVS or Walgreens and buying Sleep-Aid. According to the directory, the nearest 24-hour pharmacy is—get this—in Inuvik. So I lay on the stiff mattress, shivering. The room was drafty. A sharp arctic gust wriggled in through the microscopic pores in the window's flaking sealant. The furnace knocked like a flattened tire. All that work it seemed to be doing, yet it wasn't producing any heat.

I could think happy thoughts, of course. Sometimes it worked, so long as I focused on the right subject matter. In college, after I'd sworn off alcohol and drugs and had to train myself to sleep without any chemical aides, I'd discovered that I was more likely to doze off if I thought about sex. Perhaps it was the repetitive motion of an imagined blowjob? Or the unencumbered joy of fantasy, the bliss of feeling my most perverted desires freed from their shackles?

I considered lulling myself to sleep with sexual imagery. But if I imagined *us*, the scene wouldn't last long. I'd feel guilty about drawing satisfaction from envisioning our union, when, at the moment, we couldn't be farther apart.

Kirsten Dunst, I thought. The pretty, all-American girl next door. I saw her rip her shirt open, the silver buttons popping off one by one and chattering against the floor like a handful of dropped dimes. Her eyes examining me with scorching intent. Her panties darkening with moisture.

Stop! I thought. Would this fantasy not invite the same guilty ruminations? I'd be cheating, and I'd feel horrible about it.

I got out of bed. I tied my shoes in the dark. I threw my sweater on. It was backwards. The tag flapped against my Adam's apple. If anyone asked why my sweater was on backwards—and who, other than myself, would be up at this hour?—I'd tell him that that's what we do in Ohio. I'd attribute the fashion trend to some made-up indie band. The Wisest Platoon.

When I'd checked into the Fort McPherson Traveler's Lodge earlier, I'd noticed a piano in the lobby. Other than sexual fantasy, there's no better way to diffuse restless energy than to make music.

Consider, again, your revised childhood. Imagine yourself wandering into your family's music room, flashlight in hand, your slippers gliding on the tile floor, and the hissing sound of your cautious, little steps.

Your parents would not tolerate late-night Debussy. They'd buy you a digital keyboard and headphones. Three, four, five nights a week, you'd struggle through jazz chords. Finally, you'd change your practice habits. You'd write songs. You'd discover that songs emerge from that same sacred frequency where we compose visions of sexual fulfillment. You'd feel freedom and bliss. You'd write lyrics. What would you say, Elizabeth? Would you tatter off poetic, pastoral images, or would you shape your most hideous thoughts into melodies? Would you confess something? Or would you hide?

"Do you mind if I play the piano?" I said to the attendant at the front desk. She'd been nodding off, presumably, until I'd come downstairs. She rubbed her eyes.

"I'd tell you 'no' if other guests are here."

"Are there other guests?"

"You are the guest."

"Then I can play the piano?"

"Yes."

"I'm not going to keep you awake, am I?"

She glared.

"It was a joke."

I crossed the lobby and lifted the piano's key guard. There was a John Denver songbook on the piano's music stand. I sat on the bench, straightened my spine, and stretched out my cold fingers. I played a C chord. The piano needed a tuning.

She called across the room, "Do you perform the requests?"

"What do you have in mind?"

"You will perform Bach. 'Air on a G String.'"

"I can't play Bach. I can't play much of anything, really. Just chords."

She glazed her lips with balm and puckered them for a moment. "You will perform old Genesis."

"I can probably figure out how to play 'Invisible Touch.'"

"That is not old Genesis. Old by now, yes, but new when it was not old."

"I understand," I said. "Here, I've got one for you. It's by a band from my hometown, Cincinnati. They're called My Helicopter Heart."

Her expression was blank, but I continued, "They hit it big a few years ago. My band opened for them one night. Before they became superstars."

"Superstars," she said.

I looked back at the piano. I pounded on the opening C minor seventh chord for six beats, then jumped down to A major for two. I repeated the sequence four times, building the intensity until the abrupt four-beat rest. Then, softly, I arpeggiated an E major chord and hummed the verse's melody. I didn't know the lyrics—nobody did. As I approached the chorus, I tensed my muscles and threw my weight into the chords. I sang the discernible lyrics, "Julie I'm sad. Julie I'm afraid. Julie we're so terrible. So terrible. Julie we're sick. Julie we're small. Julie we're so horrible. So horrible."

My rendition lacked the original version's sonic shit storm. I sounded puny and impotent. The thrash-emo genre was not compatible with solo piano; it was impossible to capture My Helicopter Heart's animal-shelter-on-fire sound. Halfway through the second verse, I stopped. Embarrassed, I glanced back at the attendant. She had headphones on and was busy surfing the Internet.

I spent the next thirty minutes composing a song. While noodling with different chord shapes, the John Denver book slipped off the music stand and struck my wrist.

Perry Farmsmith, the author of *The Ultimate Key to Quantum Consciousness*, purports that the past is always embedded in the present. Events emit echoes that radiate in all directions, propagate indiscriminately through the past, present, and future. Do you recall how when I slammed the key guard on your fingers, a songbook fell to the floor?

Sitting at the piano, I felt guilty again. But I wasn't ruminating on the key guard incident. We've discussed that enough. There was something else on my mind, another memory, another secret, which I swore I'd never confess. Since leaving, I'd successfully convinced myself that my greatest transgression had never happened; I'd evaded it at all costs, but now, here was an echo I couldn't outrun. The heinous act looped in my brain, ceaselessly.

I tried to distract myself. I looked at the piano and thought about how the Fort McPherson Traveler's Lodge needed to hire someone to refurbish it. The black paint was chipping away. The piano wobbled on its weather-warped legs. The foot pedals lay inert, disabled. Several keys had gotten stuck after I'd pressed them. It was salvageable, though. Your father, animator of dead pianos, had seen greater tragedies, sacred objects so terribly desecrated that it'd take months, even years, to restore them. But always, always, they'd rise from the dead, imbued with double the vigor and vitality they'd once possessed.

My unwanted thought was still there. Never before has an intrusive memory been so persistent in its effort to avoid suppression.

I put my fingers on the piano's keys, hoping that music would make it go away. I played an F# minor. Eb major. Ab major. Though conventional, the chords sounded *right*. It was the piano; its beaten and bruised timbre, its cries for consolation unlocked from its mangled-wood prison. I cycled through the three chords again, and on the fourth round, when I opened my mouth to sing, I emitted a painful screech. At that moment, the terrifying memory's entire spectrum of undiluted sensual data unlatched in my mind. I could hold it back no more. Averting this memory would be as futile as trying to run away from my feet. I relived its details: the air was thick with ozone, like after a thunderstorm passes; my knees throbbed from the change in atmospheric pressure; an ache in my neck; a few brave crickets chirped in the wet grass outside, perhaps telling their more reluctant friends not to worry, the storm wouldn't double-back this time. My throat was dry with the bitter aftertaste of instant coffee and chalky nicotine lozenges.

Elizabeth, I have a secret. I'm not talking about my childhood psychodrama anymore. I'm not talking about an occasional sniff of Ritalin, a monthly perusal of footfetish. com, a post-*Fast Food Nation* Big-Mac relapse, or how I keyed-up some asshole tailgater's SUV in the Kroger parking lot. This is the kind of secret that could ruin a marriage.

My hands hovered over the piano keys. I glanced at the attendant. She was asleep, her head hanging back and mouth wide open. She was snoring now, music still emanating from her headphones. I cleared my throat and confessed. I didn't feel any better afterwards.

You're thinking, "This isn't fair. Just tell me." I agree. But I'm afraid that if I start telling you the truth, I'll never finish because I'll have a nervous breakdown during the process. In other words, I'm not ready yet. I'm waiting for the right moment, and I know, I absolutely know, that I must get to Inuvik in order for that to happen. Just like Don Donovan: his transformation couldn't have happened anywhere else. So long as I'm still the same person I was yesterday and the day before, I'm going to remain incapable of honesty. This confession— it's only one that the new Wally can tell. I'm going to try to get some sleep now.

August 5

I'm back on the Dempster Highway. Sort of. I've pulled over onto the shoulder for a little bit because I'm feeling panicky. Sorry about the handwriting, my hand is half-numb. I don't know how much farther away Inuvik is because the signs are covered in snow and mud. All morning, the Honda was thumping and jerking, bottoming out, launching gravel, slush, and muck in all directions. The transmission kept struggling to free itself from second gear. I'm hesitant to move ahead because my map warns me that there are no emergency medical services on this part of the highway. The bad shocks, the half-flat tires, and the ceaseless rapping of the car's underside against the ground have revived my pre-existing back problems. At this intensity, no amount of Tylenol can alleviate the inflammation. Actually, I'm losing feeling in my arms and legs, which means that my vertebrae are crunched together and clamping down on my nerves.

There's a campground ahead. Every tent in the field is blue and bears the name Fort McPherson Tent & Canvas Factory. A few scattered fire pits send up coils of black smoke, and I wonder why anyone would want to sleep outside in this weather. Just north of the campground, along Frog Creek Road, men are fishing. They wear thin flannel jackets, baseball caps, and no gloves. The people up here don't feel cold.

The air is damp, and the clouds hovering ten feet above the ground shift shapes in the breeze. Their gray bellies roll upwards toward their white beards; their ivory fingers stretch and detach.

My driver's window kept getting glazed with dew, which froze as I headed into the wind. I'd click on the wipers, and seconds later the glass would be covered again. At one point, the mist was so thick that the Dempster Highway vanished. Since there are no markers or rails on the side of the road, I listened for the sound of gravel under the wheels. Whenever the crunching stopped, I knew I was veering off the road.

———————

My hands are still shaking. I can't feel my left leg and my fingertips. The hazard lights are clicking arhythmically, as if the car, too, is deteriorating. I feel a panic attack spinning up my spine, in through my ribs and lungs, and toward my heart from all sides. Back at home, there's a bottle of clonazepam in the cabinet above the sink. It's the anti-anxiety medication that Dr. Dillman prescribed me. I should have brought it with me, but I hadn't anticipated any panic.

———————

I'm on the Mackenzie River ferry. The water is shining gold in the sunlight, the kind of picturesque image that would make your heart shudder. I personally don't give a damn about pretty things anymore. The river could be flowing with blood, diarrhea, and eyeballs for all I care.

When I first pulled up to the ferry, a woman waiting on the deck signaled for me to roll down my window. I drove up the ramp and alongside her. She said something in another language. I told her I was American, that I only spoke one language. "Oh," she said. "I was telling you that the weather is better north. Bad snow south."

"A lot of fog," I said.

"Sog?"

"Fog," I said. I waved my hands around, like they were fog. I failed to convey anything informative.

"Fog?"

"Clouds on the ground."

She smiled. "Oh, clouds."

I didn't like having the window open. My cheeks were burning, lips becoming chapped. My heart was still thrashing from the panic attack.

She said, "We wait longer."

"We wait?"

"We wait longer for cars and trucks, and then we cross the river."

"Oh," I said. "Can I close my window? I'm cold."

"Please meet the captain and take his picture." She held out a camera. "We will show it on Myspace."

"What?" I said.

"The captain. Will you meet the captain?"

"Um," I said. "Sure." Although her request made little sense, I figured that the people up here probably had their own kinds of superstitions, like we do in America. Maybe in their culture, one mustn't cross a river without shaking hands with the ferryman or else...the boat sinks, a family member dies, a village starves, grandma gets pregnant.

I unbuckled my seatbelt and got out of the car. I collapsed.

"I'm fine, I'm fine," I said, pulling myself up by the car's door handle. I explained, "My leg fell asleep, that's all. Too much driving." The truth was, our non-ergonomic car had crippled my posture so much that my appendages lost their functionality. My spine felt mangled, my hips unhinged.

I limped across the deck to a flight of white, metal stairs. I contemplated the steep incline for a moment. "Good exercise," she said, chuckling nervously.

"Let me get this right. You want me to take a picture with the captain?"

"For Myspace. Yes. You will tell everyone you loved the Mackenzie Ferry."

"Right," I said. Despite the pain I'd have to go through in order to take a snapshot of the captain, I didn't want to offend her or debase her entire belief system. I clutched the banister and began my torturous ascent. The creaking in my knees sounded like an old barn door pulled open for the first time since the Civil War. The stairs froze the bottom of my feet, and the chill rose up my legs. My calves swelled. With each step, my anger toward the woman intensified. Did she really introduce everyone to the captain? What if the ferry was full? What if each car and truck contained more than four passengers? You could fit at least fifteen cars on this thing. Did they just skip over some people, like children and the elderly? Couldn't they just put their crazy superstitions aside for an injured American? And what was with this picture-taking nonsense? Christ, why couldn't she just leave me alone? Because she wanted me to be in pain. It was her fault that my knees throbbed, that my hands were freezing on the banister, and I'd probably never play piano or write another drama again because the doctors would have to amputate my fingers. She wanted my ears to get frostbite. She wanted my ice-coated lungs to close up. She wanted to see this dumb white American tumble down the stairs and shatter on the deck like a brittle vase—this vapid jerk on a joyride, this pale idiot who'd stupidly drove his little blue Honda to her sacred home, thinking that he could spread his virus-like oppressive capitalistic ideology to the farthest regions of the world, where natives ate raw fish plucked by hand from the river, where primates wore skinned bear and banged stones together to make fires. Yes, she wanted to see me convulse in pain, my body thrashing against the deck, my mouth begging for America. She wanted to take a picture of me busted up and post it on the Internet. She hated my culture. She hated my ethnic heritage. She hated men.

I swung around and said, "You're a smelly cunt! Fuck you!"

Silence. A white flag above the helm station flapped in the wind. She clenched her jaw. At her sides, her fingers stretched open and then curled into fists. She understood me.

"Please go back to your car," she said, pointing down the five stairs we'd ascended. "You will not meet the captain."

And now I stare at the other side of the river as it approaches. I've crossed into the Arctic Circle, the last stretch of this journey.

"Cunt" is your least favorite word. I've always respected your disdain for that foul utterance—so much, in fact, that I've prohibited myself from saying it, even when you're not around. I have no justification for why I said it to the woman, other than the possibility that this trip has ruined my mind.

There are two concrete towers sticking out of the water. On the other side of the river, there are construction vehicles, thick coils of iron cable, and stacks of steel beams. The government is building a bridge. A bridge would abolish the need for a ferry. That might explain why the woman wanted me to take a picture with the captain, to post it on the Internet, and to tell everyone that I had a great time on the Mackenzie River Ferry. She didn't want to lose her job. I'm such an ass.

I have arrived in Inuvik. I feel like all my cells are finally falling into place after thirty-two years of being shaken up. Not that I *belong* here or could ever thrive in such an environment; this is the kind of place where it's so cold that they have to keep their sewer systems above ground. Some houses have windows facing the poop-pipelines. Had I been raised here, I'd have the constant reminder that everyone shits. I would have spent my youth pondering whose turds just zipped by.

Honestly, Elizabeth, I was expecting igloos. How wrong I was. The main drag, Mackenzie Road, has souvenir and antique shops, like a New England town. They've got a beatnik café and a chiropractor, who I should probably visit. Then there's the Inuvik Family Centre. It has bowling lanes and an indoor waterslide. There's a McDonald's. Aside from the language and ice barrier, this is a fairly Americanized town, but I didn't get to explore much.

Here's the part that I'm reluctant to tell you. I spent a few hours in a one-floor hospital, throwing up again and again. The sickness arose from exhaustion, dehydration, and back pain so debilitating that they gave me Soma, which is a euphoria-producing muscle relaxant. I'm fine, though. I just needed medical attention for minor nerve damage, nothing permanent. I didn't even have to pay a hospital bill. The common good took care of me.

The Inuvik Family Hospital has its own pharmacy located at the other end of the wing. I had to wait fifteen minutes for the pharmacist to fill the order, so I sat in one of the three chairs against the wall next to a young female who had her legs crossed. She wore hiking boots, but they were old, their soles hanging and shoelaces frayed. She'd put on so much lipstick that her lips looked like wrapped sausages. She wore layers of mascara. She said something in a language that I didn't understand.

"Sorry," I said. "I speak English."

"Oh, you're American?" Her voice was clotty, phlegm rattling in her throat like a stopped-up drain. She was definitely ill.

"Yes. From Ohio," I said.

"I'm Russian," she said. She tossed her blond hair over her shoulder. "I'm a hooker."

"You mean a tourist, right?"

She shook her head. "No. A hooker."

"That's wonderful." I stared straight ahead at a rotating book rack. It was mostly full of Bibles, Dan Brown, and Stephen King.

I said, "So what brings you to the pharmacy?"

I suddenly feared that I was sitting four inches away from an STD that would make my urine look like a spinach and broccoli smoothie.

"I have a tumor." She pointed to the back of her neck.

I put my hands on my knees and swallowed hard.

She said, "Why are you here?"

I said, "I needed to get away."

She pointed to my wedding ring. "From your wife?"

It was a leading question, a way for her to ensnare me. If I said, "Yes," she'd make a sexual proposition. She'd tell me that she's the kind of woman who understands. Believe me, I felt horrible about thinking this, but her tumor was questionable. It was probably a ploy, a selling point, a way to entice sympathetic perverts.

"Um," I said.

"Does she hurt you?"

"No. She's a good person. It's me, really. I'm the problem."

"Then you should go back home and say you are sorry." Her shining lips broke into a smile.

I said, "The thing is, I've made it this far, and besides—"

She interrupted, "I had a husband in Volgograd for five years. When the tumor came, he went away and never came back. I look for Danil, but cannot find him. Last year, his sister said he stay in Yellowknife. I come here and searched and searched, but I cannot find him, and I have become very sick. Now, I go home. You say you are sorry to your wife, OK? Do it for me."

I dug my fingers into my legs. "She won't want to hear it."

"I forgive Danil. What does that say?"

"It says that Russians are more understanding than Americans."

The pharmacist called her name. I couldn't even try to pronounce it if I tried. Before she walked to the counter, she leaned over my lap and said, "I hope you find what you look for. I will tell you this: it's not in Inuvik. It's not for me, it's not for you, it's not for anyone. Go home and tell your wife you love her. When a hooker tells you to be good to your wife…"

And now I'm checked into the Mackenzie Hotel. The room is small. There's one hanger in the closet. There are no brochures or pamphlets or complimentary bags of tea. There isn't a Bible in the nightstand drawer.

My plan is that, in a few minutes, I'll go down to the hotel bar, appropriately called the Mad Trapper. I'm going to meet Santa. He'll be there because I want him to be there. If you can think a B-Gravitrope into existence, then I can conjure Santa Claus.

This is going to work, Elizabeth.

———————

How do I even begin to explain what has happened? I feel so… I don't even want to write this. If I could snap this pen over my knee and throw this bundle of letters out the window, I would. But I have to tell you what went down; I owe it to you. Let me walk you through the events.

I lounged in a booth at the Mad Trapper for hours. At what I guessed was midnight, a man with a white beard entered. His stomach was so large that he couldn't button his flannel. He sat with a group of laborers and chain-smoked and chatted for half an hour. I ate three hamburgers and took two Soma pills. Although my motor skills were depressed, my thoughts were unaffected. Soon, the men left, but he stayed. This was my moment. I approached his table.

His eyebrows tilted as I slid a chair out. I reached for his cigarette in the ashtray, took a long drag, then put it back. It was my first puff in six years. "Do you speak English?" I said, exhaling smoke.

"Who are you?" he said. His eyes narrowed.

Of course I lied. "My name is Wally. I went to Harvard. I did my post-doc at MIT. I'm a research scientist at the University of Cincinnati. I fly to universities and give lectures on dark matter. I came here to do a seminar on the dangers of believing books that unite spirituality and quantum physics."

"Are you drunk?" he said.

"I'm on drugs."

He paused, his expression hardening. "What do you want?"

I said, "I just want friendly conversation." I took his cigarette again. It was now mine.

I invited him to explain himself. He probably felt so awkward that he couldn't think of anything else to do but continue conversing.

His name was Michael. He'd been a naval officer for thirty years, had worked at Inuvik's Naval Radio Station intercepting signals from Russia. He could hear everything. After the collapse of the Soviet Union and the consequent decrease in government subsidies, he retired and became an electrical technician. He was now the only person in Inuvik who could fix a broken radio. He had the power to terminate silence.

I said, "When I was a child, I wanted a certain kind of cassette player that didn't play cassettes."

His hesitant, blinking eyes assured me of his discomfort; he had probably concluded that I was nuts. He lighted a cigarette. I swallowed another Soma and chased it with Coke.

"A cassette player that does *not* play?" he asked.

"It was a toy. A useless toy. A Transformer. It was supposed to fuel my imagination. It was supposed to transform me. It was supposed to herald in my parents' return from China. I was denied."

"Denied?"

I said, "I sent you clippings every week for six months. You must have listened to my grandfather. That liar."

"What are you talking about?" He giggled, and gazed around the room for someone to save him.

"Six months. 1983. Soundwave, remember?"

He shifted in his chair. Something came over his eyes, like a protective gloss. He put his finger to his bearded chin. "Oh, uh, yes. I think I remember now," he said. He was playing along and maybe wondering if I had a gun. His eyes darted to the bar and back.

I went on, "I wrote you letters. I prayed to you. I was as good as I could be, despite what Grandpa said. I even forgave him!"

"What is it that you want?"

I took another drag. He glanced at the clock on the wall. "I wanted to tell you something. That's why I drove here from Cincinnati."

"Yeah?"

I said, "You're a fat fucking piece of fucked up shit. Fuck you for fucking me up."

It took him a moment to absorb it. He repeated my words quietly to himself. He tried to conceal what was either pity or amusement. His lips quivered, and maybe he was about to inform me that I had mistaken his identity, but I could tell that he wanted this to end.

"You finished?" he asked. "I'd like to go home and see my wife."

"Me, too," I said. "I'm finished."

He put his jacket on, then rushed out, glancing at me over his shoulder.

I was thrilled. I'd planned to relax, maybe finish reading Bertrand Russell's book. I went out to the car to get my Cheez-Its, the perfect way to celebrate my release from years of oppressive childhood memories and their resultant psychic impediments. Yes, I would eat Cheez-Its, take a hot bath, and write you love sonnets.

Out in the parking lot, the air was so cold that it burned my cheeks. I followed the rows of cars until I found our Honda, opened the driver's side door, took out the crackers, and turned around to go back to the hotel.

He startled me. He hadn't even left footprints in the snow. Like your particle, he leapt into reality. It was Santa Claus. Not Michael the electrician, not some surrogate manifestation, but the cartoonish freak on Hallmark cards. He wore a red Santa hat, red clothes, black mittens and black boots. His beard looked like a ruffled-up white sweater. I flinched. I shook my head. I looked away from him, up to the amber streetlight's glow, then back, hoping he would have vanished between my glances. He remained. I dropped my box of Cheez-Its. The crackers spilled out and slid along the ice.

I said, "I think there's been a terrible misunderstanding."

His white eyebrows arched, indicating that he was humored. His mouth curved at the edges.

I said, "What the hell? This isn't real, right?"

He gawked at me, wordless.

"This is a simulation," I said. "My unconscious mind is doing it without my permission. This is a revenge fantasy that I'm supposed to walk through, right? This isn't psychosis, this is self-psychology, that's all."

Then it occurred to me that only people who are bat-shit experience therapeutic hallucinations.

He wasn't saying anything. He just studied my face, his clear blue eyes clinging to me. "Speak!" I demanded.

I took a deep breath and it hurt. I saw you in my mind, hurriedly packing your bags, stuffing boxes with old dresses and college textbooks with orange "Used Saves" stickers still on their spines. You would leave the wedding pictures on the walls. You would take the potted plants. You would take the toothpaste and the bath towels.

There was a couple walking through the parking lot toward a Ford pickup. I couldn't tell whether they were real or imagined, but they were arguing. Even Santa turned his head. The man cried, "I don't care about your feelings and inner conflicts. I just want you to behave!"

"Can't you see?" she said. "I have a problem!"

"Right, and it shouldn't be my problem. I can stomach a lot, but you've taken this too far. It's affecting me."

I gulped. She continued, "That's easy for you to say, Paul. You don't know what it's like to be sad every single day of your life." Her voice was rapid, like fingers running up and down a church organ.

Paul stomped his foot on the snow and it crunched. "You know what they used to do on the Oregon Trail when someone complained about how depressed they were feeling?"

"No. What?"

"They'd throw the person off a cliff and move on."

"What?"

He opened the car door for her. "Just get in the car. You're drunk and we're going home."

She slid into the passenger's seat. He got in and started the car. I turned to look at Santa Claus. I said, "Can you just tell me. How much of this is real?"

He said, "Merry Christmas, Wally. This is the biggest triumph of your life."

He patted me on the shoulder and disappeared.

The television in my room is broken; it receives only the snow channel. I've considered calling Michael to ask him to come fix it. My motive, of course, would be to reaffirm his status as the real Santa Claus. But I can't fool myself. I've lost my ability to interpret things. I no longer trust how my mind reads the world. I have achieved nothing, not even a semblance of the hyper-objective Peter Prynne mentality. If I were to write a journal entry, it wouldn't be anything like his. It'd be long, so fucking long. I sure as hell couldn't compose one simple sentence about a displeasing apple.

It's clear to me now what has held back my transformation. I haven't been honest. I've evaded every opportunity to confess my secret. I'm not just terrified of your response; I'm reluctant to acknowledge a part of me that I cannot live with.

The way the psyche tries to suppress autobiographical events is fascinating. Although the mind's strategies and coping mechanisms have proven ineffective time and time again throughout our lives, we allow our brains to repeatedly take up these broken tools. It's like finding a well-reputed contractor to replace your shingles, then deciding to hire a handyman who's got a reputation for caving-in roofs instead. Suppressing thoughts actually empowers them.

A while back, Dr. Dillman once explained to me the process of memory rebound. Simply put, when we try not to think about a trauma, our repeated act of denial becomes a continual recognition of the trauma's presence. The harder we fight it, the stronger it becomes. Even worse, if we try to distract ourselves by thinking about something else, our minds break in two: one part focuses on the distraction, and the other assesses whether the distraction has successfully inhibited the unwanted thought. A fragmented mind becomes neurotic.

I can no longer distract myself, nor can I continue to justify withholding my secret. My resistance paradoxically imbues the memory with power and vitality. I'm immobilized, my eyes pried open so that I can do nothing but watch my memory's cyclical playback, its loyalty to uncontaminated, un-revisable realism, its agonizing precision, its scornful objectivity, its message reinforced and replicated unrelentingly. If I don't tell you the truth, I will commit the crime again and again.

Here it is, Elizabeth. Breathe heavily. Know that I'm breathing heavily, too. We're breathing together. I'm holding your hand because I love you, and I never meant you any harm.

After the key guard incident, I promised you I'd change. Although we attended therapy and I switched to "better" medication, my problems remained. I kept my instability guarded. I put up a convincing façade. I had everyone fooled. During the four years since the key-guard incident, I've given a Tony Award-worthy performance of sanity. Our domestic life: the best play I've ever written. But there's one problem. The show is always over after five acts.

Ten days ago, I entered the forbidden sixth act, where truth terminates the fantasy of tidy endings. It was my turn to cook. I made tofu burritos. They came out too wet and sloppy, the beans leaking from the sides, the tomatoes splattering against our plates. You found my culinary ineptitude entertaining. It was proof that I was the worst chef you'd ever met. But you ate my terrible meal anyway. As you bit into it, the uncontainable red juices dripped over your lower lip, and the steam coiled out from the burrito's side. Your face tightened, as if you'd just taken a shot of bourbon. You said, "Woo, that's bitter."

Outside, the thunder grumbled. The storm was far off now. I felt an ache in my knees.

You swallowed, and I watched the lump move down your esophagus. You said, "Can I have some water? My throat feels raw."

I said, "Too many jalapeños I guess. Next time I'll use more cheese."

As I reached for the water pitcher, I felt a crick in my neck.

You slurped down your water, then took another bite of the burrito. You were being courteous; you didn't want me to feel like a failure. You ate the whole darned thing in three, wide-mouthed chomps. I wanted to stop you but my body seized, and my brain, so shocked from what I'd done, went into trauma paralysis. You chugged two more glasses of water. A glaze of sweat formed beneath your hairline. You stood and wiped your forehead with a napkin. "Way too many spices, Wally. I need to take a break. I need to go sit by the window and get fresh air."

You sat in the recliner. I pulled one of your Star Trek DVDs off the shelf and loaded it up.

"I feel really sick," you said, your voice hoarse.

I eyed the telephone on the other side of the room in case I'd need to call 911.

"My stomach," you moaned, palm pressed against your belly button. "It's like I drank battery acid. I feel like I'm going to puke. You're not feeling the same thing?"

"I feel a little off, but maybe that's because I'm tired."

Outside, a few crickets chirped.

I said, "Should I call the doctor?"

You shook your head. "Probably minor food poisoning. Maybe the tomatoes were too old?"

"I'm sorry."

"I'm not blaming—"

And then you retched, an orange tsunami of burrito slime and water. You gagged for a minute straight, heaving so loud and hard that the blood vessels in your eyes popped one by one, like a string of firecrackers. I leaned over you, my hand on the small of your back. As you gasped, I glanced at the puddle. I was looking to see if there was any blue powder floating among your upchucked refuse. I figured the powder had enough time to dissolve, but you can never be sure. Were I to discover a single grain of the Ajax I'd sprinkled inside your burrito, I'd rush to the utility closet and grab a mop and bucket. Get rid of the evidence. But all the Ajax was gone. It was now inside of you, tearing up your stomach, your kidneys becoming enflamed, your liver shriveling.

Elizabeth, I poisoned you. I'd used just a pinch of the stuff. Certainly not enough to kill you. That's not what I wanted. I don't know what I wanted. I can't even say that it was me doing it.

I imagine you're saying, "I want to know why you did this to me, damn it! What went through your head?"

I'll tell you. The Ajax was on the counter, where you'd left it a week ago, after cleaning the refrigerator. I picked it up. Here's exactly what I thought: "I'm going to put Ajax in her food."

I wasn't feeling hatred toward you. I wasn't feeling resentful over Kyle. Things were going just fine. Something came over me.

You once told me about an experience you'd had while playing a Debussy nocturne on the piano. You were seventeen. Your parents were gone for the evening, at a church function.

Your brother had left an hour prior for a Magic tournament. You went down to the music room, candles cradled in your arms. Then, surrounded by the flickering amber glow, you sat before the Steinway grand. You felt a breeze move through you. Something transcendent had happened. Your hands lifted, descended upon the keys, and seemed to move on their own accord. You played with a level of grace and passion that, I quote, you were "incapable" of producing on your own. "I could have walked away, and the piano would have kept playing," you described. "I've never believed in the Holy Spirit, but that experience opened my mind to the possibility."

I'll tell you this: the breeze that moved through me, Elizabeth, was not the Holy Spirit.

My great-grandfather Owen died when Marvin was a teenager. I know almost nothing about Owen but for two things: he fought for the Union in the Civil War and, when Marvin was a baby, Owen had taken him out of the crib one winter night and thrown him on the front lawn. Apparently, Marvin cried a lot, and Owen could no longer take it. We can assume that Owen had done similarly horrific things to Marvin in the subsequent years. I wonder if Marvin was a good child, an innocent, imaginative, and sympathetic child. On the day Owen died, did Marvin feel a shiver? Did he feel not quite himself after, and for the rest of his life? Had the demon left the father for the son?

I remember my father's face when he got the phone call about the fire at Marvin's condo. I'd walked in the door a half-hour prior, my eyes feeling greasy from Visine, Iron Maiden shirt stinking of cologne, and breath potent with spearmint candies. I was planning on doing my homework. My father held the phone to his ear and stared across the living room.

He said, "I see." He said it over and over again. "I see. I see. I see." Then, he hung up. He rubbed his eyes, but there weren't any tears.

"Who was that?" I said.

He stood. "I'm going over to Grandpa's. Get your driver's permit. You're coming with me. You might need to drive on the way home."

I wondered if someone had discovered the pinholes I'd jabbed into Marvin's leg, if I was walking into a trap, if the police were waiting there for me. But then, Dad said, "There's been a fire."

As he drove to Bergen County, he was silent. Then, at a red light, he began to cry.

There were three fire trucks and numerous police cruisers and ambulances outside the condo. A crowd of onlookers stood across the street, their faces flashing in the sweeping red and white lights. Dad pulled up next to the fire chief. "Wait here," he said, leaving me in the idling car.

The entire building was scorched black. Thick smoke still rolled out the shattered windows. The firemen just stood around, never a good sign. I watched my father. He was talking with the chief, an old friend that he'd worked with at Engine Company 39 in Harlem. The chief shook his head forlornly. I saw my father close his eyes and turn away.

My body twitched, though it wasn't a spasm or a painful muscle contraction. The only analogous sensation that comes to mind is, well, the feeling you get when you lie on polyurethane, that moment when your body surrenders its tension to the mattress. You feel the surface shaping itself around you, adapting to your form, making accommodations for all your awkward angles and jutting bones. I wonder if our polyurethane comforts come not from corporeal pleasantries, but from our selfish love of our own images impressed and preserved on the mattress. Whether we're seduced by its elastic snugness or its complicity to our vainglorious fervor, the moment we lay down on memory foam we give up our body's borders; the polymers embrace us, neutralize our contours, amend our asymmetries, homogenize our bumpy perimeters, raze our fleshy walls, and leave us flat and exposed. We're not sheltered, we're prone.

There, in my father's idling car, I felt comfort because Marvin was dead. Maybe my willingness to sink into the illusion of comfort made me vulnerable. I twitched. It could have been a bunch of dormant, malevolent genes suddenly roused by the circumstance's emotional force. Or perhaps, when Marvin's skin melted into the mattress, when the memory foam finally consumed all of him, his spirit, now free, turned its gaze upon me.

Whatever it was, Marvin's impression stayed with me from that day on. But how could you have known?

———————

Here's what I'm thinking about: Nine years ago, when we'd been dating about a year, you drove down to Syracuse to visit me for the weekend. I'd just been fired from my job at Whole Foods for failing to show up three days in a row. I'd been busy writing a play about Peter Prynne, which, at the time, seemed more important than paying the bills.

You sat on my mattress. I didn't have a couch or any seats other than the one at my computer, which was piled high with books about the English Civil War. I held the manuscript in my hand and stood above you.

"The thing is," I said, "I don't want to give people the wrong impression about Peter by attributing to him characteristics that aren't accurate."

"It's a play," you said. "Not a History Channel documentary. You're worrying too much."

"Right. But I can't let myself get out of control. I need some balance between fiction and fact. The problem is Peter is so hard to read. In his journals, he presents himself as such a bland guy. Even the subtext is so ambiguous that it's impossible to create an objective estimate of what he was thinking. For instance—" I rushed to my computer seat and pulled his journal out from the middle of the pile. The rest of the books toppled onto the floor.

I thumbed through a few pages. You cleared your throat, adjusted your shirt so that a little more of your cleavage was showing.

I read: "April 5, 1592. The pigeons have returned. There are fewer. When the rain clears, I expect more. April 14, 1592. The pigeons have left. I have gone to the glover. The market was crowded. It has not rained for three days."

You slipped your sneakers off and wiggled your toes, perhaps hoping I'd become aroused by your feet. I continued reading, "April 16, 1592. Alfred not feeling well again. Walking this morning, I came across a dead fox in the woods. The weather was fair, though moist. April 22, 1592. The weather was fair, though moist. Alfred is in better spirits. I could not find my gloves again."

You stood. Your expression was stern.

"Wally," you said. "Are we going to have sex or not?"

"Hold on," I said. "One more passage."

You grabbed the book.

I became angry. I felt my face tighten. I gave you a look, one you'd never seen before, one that I'd never felt myself give to anyone. It didn't belong on my face. It scared you, made you avert your gaze. For a moment, you didn't feel safe. You had met the ghost of my dead grandfather.

I said, "Don't ever fucking do that again."

Part of me wished that you would have done anything other than apologize, but you were terrified. I wish you would have said, "I've never heard you talk that way. I didn't even know you were capable of it. My God, Wally. What's gotten into you?"

I would have explained it, maybe.

Elizabeth, I'll come home now, but I want you to know I'm scared. I have a feeling that when I arrive, you'll be in the middle of packing your belongings. Or, even worse, I'll find a moving company doing the job for you. I'll discover a note taped to the shower curtain. It'll say, "Wally, I'm someplace safe right now. Don't try to find me. I'm not coming back." Both scenarios are unlikely because, by the time these letters arrive, I'll be driving through Toledo. Maybe if I only stop to rest when it's absolutely necessary, I might get to Cincinnati within an hour from now. That way, you'll be able to see, in person, that this trip has helped me. It's made me honest. I hope you'll have the chance to look into my eyes and think to yourself, "It's true. He's different. He's a good man now."

Please, for the love of God, please be there. There's a lot that we *must* talk about if we're going to move ahead in our lives together. The most important issue involves something that, for the life of me, I can't figure out on my own, and it would make all the difference in the world if I could. I tried to solve the dilemma; I got in the car and drove all the way up here hoping to lay the issue to rest. But it seems I'm chasing a question only you can answer.

Is he dead, Elizabeth? Is he? Just tell me that he's dead.

About the Author

Don Peteroy lives with his wife in Cincinnati, Ohio. His short story, "The Circuit Builders," won first place in the Playboy College Fiction Contest, and was published in the October 2012 issue. Other stories have appeared, or are forthcoming, in *Cream City Review, Permafrost, Eleven Eleven, Chattahoochee Review, Santa Clara Review, Yemassee*, and elsewhere. He is a PhD candidate at the University of Cincinnati. He blogs at letterstojamesfranco.com.

Acknowledgments

Thanks to the following:

Ryan Rivas and the rest of Burrow Press for supporting me, and helping me make this book the best it can be.

My wife, Phoebe Reeves, for her hot love and support, and for vacuuming up all the hair I've ripped out of my head since I started writing this book.

My father for becoming a man of honor, for introducing me to the love of my life: literature, and for being supportive of all my crazy, oftentimes dimwitted ventures.

My mother and sister for their faith and patience during my dimwitted ventures.

My in-laws for their unquestionable enthusiasm, love, and devotion.

Seth Courtwright, who encouraged me not to abandon this story, and proved to be a great friend.

Chris Wendl, the great mathematician and physicist, who was essential toward the creation of this book.

David James Poissant for providing amazing critiques, and useful insight and inspiration.

And, especially, my mentors, professors, and peers at the University of Cincinnati who assisted me along the way: Leah Stewart, Michael Griffith, Chris Bachelder, Brock Clarke, and Dr. Jonathan Kamholtz.

CPSIA information can be obtained at www.ICGtesting.com
Printed in the USA
LVOW060617200912

299567LV00004B/1/P